INTIMATE NIGHT

DARK ATTRACTION BOOK TWO

DRAKE LAMARQUE

A catalogue record for this book is available from the National Library of New Zealand.

978-1-7385967-6-8 kindle

978-1-7385967-7-5 epub (wide)

978-1-7385967-8-2 paperback

PREFACE

1

BRANDON

I changed my shirt for the third time and eyed myself in the mirror. Pale green Oxford shirt with a pattern of blue flowers. I'd worn it maybe once before and I liked the way the green made my tanned skin glow, but was it nice enough?

"Hey Max!" I called.

A thump came from the next room of our small apartment and then my best friend responded.

"Yeah?"

"Is this place like, jacket and tie fancy?"

There was a pause while he considered this.

"No, it's more like hipster fancy!"

"Thanks!"

If it was hipster fancy then this shirt was perfect.

I could do this.

I could have a pleasant birthday dinner with the three most important people in my life. It would be fun.

Wouldn't it?

I wasn't the kind to get nervous, but something about having dinner in a nice restaurant with my older sister, my best friend (who had recently started dating my sister) and my vampire dom of a boyfriend had me sweating and second-guessing my choices. Maybe it wasn't too late to call it all off?

I checked my phone for the time and swore. "We have to get going."

"Well, yeah man, I've been waiting for you." Max appeared in the doorway to my room, clean and fresh in a crisp blue linen shirt with rolled up sleeves and loose pants. He looked like the CEO of some new Silicon Valley startup.

"Fine, then let's get out of here." I pocketed my phone and wallet and followed Max down to the car.

"You okay? You seem kind of … wired." Max looked at me sidelong before starting the car.

"Yeah, just." I took a breath. "I really want you to like Gage, and I don't know what your first impression of him is going to be."

"If you like him he must be a good guy," Max said. "So just chill. Martina and I are cool people, you're cool, I'm sure he's cool too. Iit'll be cool."

I swallowed, comforted despite the number of times Max had said the word 'cool'. Was he nervous as well?

"Thanks Max."

———

Max pulled up outside a concrete wall with a restaurant name stenciled next to an unassuming door.

"*Lot 17*? This really is hipster."

Max chuckled. "Martina read about it online. Apparently it'll blow our minds."

"It looks like we'll be sitting on benches in a cold concrete cell, but sure."

Someone emerged from the door before we even got close. She had a clipboard in hand and blond hair that feathered around her face.

"Names please."

"Max Hoffman, table for four." Max gave me a reassuring nod.

"Right this way. One of your party is already here," the hostess said.

I swallowed. Would Gagle be prickly about being kept waiting?

The inside of the restaurant was nothing like its sterile exterior. It was pretty, painted white with lots of house plants and lamps dotted around. The tables and chairs were all vintage mis-matched wood. There were partitions everywhere, as if the place was made up of dozens of cozy, well-designed living rooms smashed together in one building.

Martina sat at a table for four. She stood up to give me a warm hug.

"Happy birthday, baby brother."

"Thanks, Marty." I squeezed her against me. Of my closest family, it was always my sister who kept tabs on me, who looked after me. She was my best friend after Max.

But I still looked away as they kissed hello.

Max took the seat beside her and I sat opposite, leaving the remaining chair for Gage.

"So, how are you?" Martina leaned her chin on her hand.

"I'm good, really good. A bit nervous about how tonight will go but I'm hopeful."

"You think we're going to embarrass you in front of your boyfriend?" Max teased.

"No, it's just. Gage's a little...unusual." How to phrase this? "He might not look how you expect, so don't jump to conclusions."

"As long as he's treating you right, he has my approval, B." Martina glanced at Max. "You've met him, right?"

Max shook his head. "Nope, just heard about him a lot."

"Shut up, I don't talk about him that much."

"You literally gush about him every time I see you." Max rolled his eyes and sipped from his glass of water. "It's adorable but also pretty annoying, honestly."

I blushed. "It's not like—"

"Are you talking about me?" Gage's voice was close.

I startled so badly I bumped my knee on the table, swiveling to look at him.

Gage had forgone his usual goth punk look for a tailored black suit, probably Armani, with a deep v-neck gray T-shirt under the jacket. He'd slicked back his bright red hair, and left most of his jewelry off. He looked like he'd stepped out of GQ magazine or off the red carpet at a movie premier.

My mouth went dry but I stood to make the introductions because otherwise I was going to go onto my knees for him right there in the restaurant.

"Gage, this is my sister Martina and my best friend Max. Guys, meet Gage."

Once Gage had shaken hands with them both, he tugged me in for a kiss. It was smoldering hot but I broke it off before it got *too* steamy.

"Happy birthday," Gage said. He ruffled my hair as I sat down.

"Thanks." I picked up the menu, my mind utterly blank for things to say.

Martina cleared her throat. "So, Gage, Brand tells us you're not in college?"

"That's right, I have my own business." Gage looked over the wine menu. "But we met at a campus party. I'm still friends with my fraternity little brothers so I drop in on them now and then."

"Sweet of you," Max said.

"So, you run your business. What do you do?" Martina flicked through the menu then shut it, fixing Gage with a piercing look.

"Lots of different things. App design, bit of buying and

4

selling, playing the stock markets, you name it." Gage smiled. Lying came naturally to him — of course it did with what he was. He was constantly lying that he was an ordinary person.

"That's impressive." Martina looked straight at him. "Is it a career though?"

Gage hesitated, his eyes narrowing ever so slightly.

I wanted to step in, interrupt but I wasn't sure how to.

Was Martina really going to do the protective family member thing? Interrogate him to make sure he was 'worthy' enough to date me?

"So far it's going great." Gage leaned forward on his forearms.

My stomach knotted, suddenly afraid of what he might say.

"I'm planning to expand the buying and selling, open an online megastore, then a warehouse. Hire people to fulfill orders, that sort of thing. In the long run, I'm thinking of an Amazon-style business with more reach, more antiques and luxury items and workers who are paid a decent wage with lots of benefits."

My eyes widened. This was news to me. Was this the actual plan or was just bullshitting to sound good to Martina?

Either way it worked. Martina lapped it up. "Oh, I'd love it if there was an ethical competitor for Amazon. What are your plans for sustainability?"

The waitress returned to take our orders and when she left there was a moment's silence, all of us staring at each other.

Max broke the silence.

"So, Brand, we got you a present. Do you want it now?"

I silently sent him thanks, the tension was killing me.

"Of course he wants it." Martina laughed.

Max pulled out a gift bag from the floor between him and Martina and set it on the table. "Happy birthday, man."

"Thanks." I hadn't expected to receive anything, so I was genuinely surprised at the gesture. I pulled the gift bag towards me. Inside was a large, hardcover book with full-color sketches of marine wildlife from all over the globe. It was beautiful, and the thoughtfulness of it struck me.

"This is... awesome, thanks guys."

Gage set a little blue box on the table in front of me.

I put the book back in its bag and regarded the gift box. Dread pooled in my stomach.

"Gage, you didn't..."

"Go to Tiffany's? Yes I did. But don't panic, this isn't a proposal, just a birthday gift."

My stomach unknotted itself. I picked up the box, through the link I could feel that Gage was anxious now, just a touch. Worried I wouldn't like it? Or that he had picked the wrong thing entirely?

I focused on feeling as warm and pleased as possible. It wasn't hard, the book from Max and Marty was touching. Besides, knowing that Gage had gone to a luxury jewelers, and bought something for me? He not only cared enough to do that, but he thought I was worth something like this, treating me just because it was my birthday? I'd never had a relationship like that before. I loved the way it felt.

Hopefully Gage felt some of this through the empathic link that connected us.

My fingers didn't exactly shake as I undid the delicate ribbons that held the box shut, but I fumbled with it, not sure what to expect.

A thrill of terror went through me —Tiffany's didn't make cock rings did they? I counld't put it past Gage to have stuck a sex toy in a Tiffany's box to humiliate me.

But he wouldn't do that in front of my sister would he? Would he?

"Come on, Brand, I want to see what it is!" Martina whined.

I pulled the ribbon off. Inside was a velvet jewelry box.

"Oooh." Martina leaned forward. "Fancy. Gage, you're winning all kinds of points by spoiling my little brother."

From what I could pick up from our empathic link, Gage didn't feel like he was tricking. He felt really content.

My mind raced. Gage had already given me a necklace with his family crest on it, and I wore it constantly. I didn't imagine it'd be anything to wear around my neck, a leather cuff or any of the gothic stuff Gage liked to wear wouldn't have fit in the box.

I flipped the box open to find a golden ring. It looked like a little knotted string, or, I supposed rope, made of gold. The band was split in two and at the front there were two knots with little ends sticking out. It shone in the restaurant lighting.

My breath caught.

"It should fit on your right ring finger." Gage said. "I measured when you were sleeping one time." He took the box off me and slipped the ring out. I watched, stunned. No one had ever given me anything that beautiful before. My heart thudded and tears welled in my eyes. I blinked them back, swallowing a small lump in my throat.

Gage took my hand in one of his, gentler than he usually was with me. I watched as he slipped it onto my finger. It fit perfectly, because of course it did.

He really had measured my finger while I slept. I had no idea I slept that heavily but then, after one of our sessions I was usually dead to the world.

Which meant he planned this in advance. I hadn't expected that.

"Brand."

I looked up at Max. Why had he said my name?

Instead of his face, I saw Max's phone. I blushed. He was taking photos, possibly even filming. I was at once embarrassed and secretly pleased that the moment had been captured.

"Thank you." I turned my hand, admiring the way the gold

shone. Then I leaned in and gave Gage a kiss. "Really, thanks. It's so wonderful."

"You two are so cute." Martina giggled.

Gage slipped his arm around my shoulders and squeezed, keeping his eyes on my face. "Happy birthday, pup."

The food arrived then, which was lucky. Gage using any kind of pet name for me gave me inappropriate-for-being-in-public feelings.

2

BRANDON

I'd never been in Gage's car before. It was a sleek, shiny black sports car so low I practically had to fold myself in half to get into it was so low. The bucket seats were leather. It felt like being inside a rocket. The dash was covered in readouts and buttons, and from the silent way it moved, I figured it was electric.

Gage watched me as I marveled. "You like it?"

"It's a wet dream."

"I want to fuck you over the hood of it."

Gage's ability to say incredibly hot things in a completely casual way kept me off guard. I couldn't respond. I stared at the hood, my pants suddenly way too tight.

Gage pulled into traffic.

"Not tonight though, that would be a whole me arresting you scenario out in the backwaters, and it's your birthday. You get birthday sex."

"Birthday sex?" I tore my gaze from the hood of the car to look at him. "What's birthday sex?"

"Everything just for you, maximizing your pleasure as much as possible."

He drove perfectly as we talked, whereas I was sporting a half-chub and barely able to keep my breathing under control.

"How... how is that different from how we normally are? Because it feels like I get a lot of pleasure every time."

Gage chuckled. "Wait and see, puppy. I'll surprise you."

I had no doubt.

It felt like an age but couldn't have been more than a couple of minutes before we pulled into the parking garage under his building.

On the way up to his apartment he was quiet, didn't touch me or anything, no doubt enjoying the excited nervousness I radiated. I could never predict what Gage was going to do and the anticipation was somehow even worse.

When we got into the apartment he tossed his keys and wallet onto the table and turned to me. Like the puppy dog I was, I followed his lead and unloaded the gift bags, my keys and wallet onto the table.

The instant I'd done that, Gage was on me. He leaned up on his toes to kiss me, hands busy undoing my shirt buttons.

"Did you really like the ring?" His mouth found my neck.

I closed my eyes as he kissed his way up my neck.

"Yeah, I love it."

"I could give you more stuff like that, you know. I'd like to. Buy you whatever you need, shower you with gifts."

I moaned softly as he fastened his teeth onto my earlobe and gently tugged. "Sounds sorta like you want to be my sugar daddy."

He ran his ice-cold hands up my chest to rub my nipples. "Yeah. Is that a bad thing?"

I swallowed. "No, not at all. I just... we should probably set the terms of it or something. I don't want you buying me a helicopter."

He snorted against my throat and gently bit my shoulder. "Why the fuck would I buy you a helicopter?"

"I don't know, I just know I don't want one."

He pulled back, eyeing me with amusement. "Brand. I want to buy you stuff you'd actually use. Nicer versions of the clothes you have, a good suit, maybe a designer bag to take to college, fountain pens and shit. I have a ton of money and I want to spoil you."

I leaned in to kiss him, already missing the proximity. I searched my feelings as I kissed him. In some ways I felt I should refuse his offer. It wasn't like I was poor, or my family was in trouble or anything like that. But what he offered sounded really nice.

Why couldn't I say yes? He wanted to spoil me and I wanted to be spoiled, why not agree?

"Yeah." I breathed it, barely audible, against his lips.

He smiled.

"Yeah? You mean it? I'll take you shopping tomorrow if you mean it."

I took a deep breath and looked him in the eye so he could see how sincere I was. "Yes, it sounds like fun."

"Oh it will be. But first..." Gage swept me into his arms. In one movement I was over his shoulder, arms hanging down his back. He fireman-carried me to the bedroom. I laughed, mostly from surprise, but the act of being lifted, tossed around like I weighed nothing also made me even hornier.

He tossed me onto the bed and started undressing. I kicked off my pants and boxers and watched, knowing to stay still and not touch him unless he gave express permission.

Gage went to the drawer he kept his gear in and came back with a handful of silk scarves, all black and red, because of course they were.

"Scarves?" I couldn't keep the laughter out of my voice. He'd chained me before, used leather and everything. This seemed so... basic.

"Yep, don't underestimate them. Lay back."

I lowered myself to the bed, content to take orders and see

what he had planned. Gage always had a plan and it always worked out well for me.

He set the scarves down, and gently stroked his hands up my forearms, lifting them and bringing them together in front of me. "Thread your fingers together for me, pet."

I pressed my palms together and threaded my fingers.

He took one of the scarves and wound it around my wrists several times. He pulled it tight and tied a knot. Smirking, he looked down at me.

"Try and get out."

I unthreaded my fingers and tried to twist away, smiling as I did. I liked this game, we'd played it before and it had been incredibly fun and arousing. I pushed one hand up and the other down, trying to get some give, but there was nothing.

"I can't."

"That's right." Gage looped a scarf around the one on my wrists and tugged gently, lifting my arms up over my head and tying me to the bedhead.

He tied another scraf around my eyes. "You like that?"

I groaned, squirming in the darkness. "Yeah."

The removal of my sight heightened my other senses. What would he do next?

"I could gag you too, but I want to hear your noises." Gage stroked his hand down my cheek and rubbed his thumb over my lip.

I moaned. The mention of a gag aroused me so much it was as if he had gagged me. Gage knew exactly how to play me, and I reveled in it.

He moved my legs apart and tied one to each corner of the bed so my legs were entirely spread out.

"Now. I'm going to hit every one of your erogenous zones."

"You're what?"

"I have you tied up, completely at my mercy, and I'm going to do all the things I know you like." I felt his breath on my left thigh so I had a slight warning before he bit me there, a gentle bite that he followed up with sucking.

I imagined him leaving a hickey on my thigh and groaned.

"That's it, just like that. Let me hear you."

He switched to the same spot on the other thigh.

I whined, wanting to twitch away from the intensity of the sensation while also enjoying it. I loved it, but it was so much.

After a moment of that, Gage sat back. His fingers trailed over my stomach. That didn't do anything particular for me until his hands flattened out into the vee of my hips, pressing down.

He wrapped his lips around my left nipple.

I groaned, tingles shooting through my body at the attention. My right nipple got the same treatment and I groaned again, louder. He moved too quickly, getting me interested in one thing and then immediately moving on. Never quite enough in any one place.

It was the most exquisite torture I could imagine.

I wanted to beg him, to promise him anything he wanted if he'd just get on with it and fuck me, but... then he'd stop doing this, and I didn't want that either. This realization came out of me as a loud, keening whine.

"Enjoying this, pet?" It was less a question and more of a taunt.

My breath was coming so fast I wasn't sure I could respond.

Gage tapped my collarbone with one finger.

"Answer me, check in."

"Green, yeah, I'm enjoying it, how... how could I not?"

Gage's chuckle went right through me, making my rock-hard dick even more solid.

I imagined his face, the way his eyes crinkled when he smiled, the wicked twist of his lips and a wave of pure adoration washed over me. There was nothing I wouldn't do for him.

But... I didn't know how much of this I could take without

just coming unprompted, regardless of whether he touched my dick.

"Hmm, now, where else do you like? Oh yes..." His hand moved down my body, slow and serpentine, to reach between my legs and pressing against my taint. My prostate throbbed as I arched up off the bed, tugging at my restraints.

"Please!"

"You can ask better than that, pet, I know you can."

I felt the tiniest, faintest little lick of precum off the end of my dick.

My voice reached a new octave. "Please! Please sir, please fuck me and bite me, I'm so hot for you, I'll do anything."

"Don't promise things you can't deliver..." Gage's breath was on my dick.

I bucked, trying to get some friction. "I mean it, I'll do anything."

He pinned my hip with one hand.

Gage hummed. He started teasing me open, lube on his fingers. I hadn't even heard him retrieve it.

"What if I wanted to take you to a club, somewhere we could be observed. Dress you in leather and a collar and make you sit at my feet. Play with you in front of other people? Would you do that?"

The noise that came out of me in response wasn't remotely like words. I combined an aroused moan at the thought of publically being his pet with a jolt of pleasure as he pushed a finger into me up to the knuckle.

"Your dick literally twitched." Gage's tone was amused. "You like that idea."

"I, yeah, yeah I do." I grated out the words. "Please, more."

"Want to be bound in public? Leashed and me lording it over you? Because I think you'd look super hot that way. We'd be the envy of everyone else there."

Another finger. I tried my best to press against it, not an easy feat with him still holding my hips down.

"Patience puppy, always so eager for me. It's very flattering, you know, that you always want me this badly."

Part of me wanted to swear at him and demand he got on with it, but the far larger part was reveling in it. I felt his pride and his arousal, and it magnified my own need.

"Okay, I think you're ready. What do you think?"

He was pushing three fingers in and out of me and if I hadn't been tied in place I'd have been writhing.

"Yes, please sir, please."

"Call me Master and you'll have everything you want."

"Master, yes, please, please fuck me!"

With a grunt he pushed into me. He went painfully slowly, teasing out each inch as he filled me up. Reduced to panting and moaning, I tipped my head back and took it, grateful but still wildly aroused.

"I'm gonna take the blindfold off, want to see those gorgeous eyes of yours as I fuck you."

I squeezed my eyes shut, sure that the light would seem dazzling after being in the dark for so long. But it seemed he'd dimmed the room lights at some point as well. I let my eyes flutter open to look at him, my gorgeous, sexy Master. He had such a tight, toned body, pale skin practically luminous, red hair tossed back as he bottomed out inside me.

He met my eyes. I wanted to blurt out my affection, tell him how much he made me feel, how much I loved him, but I didn't need to. The connection between us was so strong, I knew he felt it.

Besides, I don't think I could have formed words because he stroked his hands up my chest and started to thrust hard.

"Maybe next time I have you like this, I'll edge you all night. Get you just to the brink and then pull back, over and over again until you're crying. How does that sound?"

I groaned, breathless.

He leaned down and kissed me hard. His fangs had popped. One of them cut my lower lip. He hummed and lapped at the blood that welled there.

"M-more..." It was the only word I could say, the only word in my whole vocabulary.

"Birthday boy, you can have more. You gonna come for me if I bite you?"

I nodded.

He started a relentless pounding rhythm with his hips, gripped my chin with one hand and sucked on my lower lip, then turned my head to the side and bit into my neck.

I would never get used to how incredible it felt when Gage drank my blood. I barely registered that he was stroking me. Every atom of me condensed down to the lush, velvet sensation of him feeding. I felt so whole, so abundant, and so... important.

Yes, part of it was the feeling of importance.

I gave him something he needed to survive. That, compounded with the fucking and my desperate arousal, and I was coming hard, gasping and moaning out my relief to the ceiling.

Gage groaned against my neck, bucking into me and filling me just as I filled him with my blood.

He pulled back and licked my neck, healing the wounds that he'd made, and slowly, ever so slowly, eased out of me.

I groaned, head flopped back to the pillow and blissed out beyond compare.

He untied me and pulled me into his arms. "Happy, birthday boy?"

"Yeah."

"Good."

3

BRANDON

A week after my birthday dinner, I made my way to Gage's apartment as the sun was going down. I carried my school backpack, a paper bag which held my afternoon snack and a paper cup holder from the bubble tea place on the corner of Gage's street. The place was called Neko Tea and had all these cute cat mascots decorating the walls. Being seen there was a little embarrassing, but the tea was so good I didn't care.

The doorman let me into Gage's building and buzzed me up in the elevator without blinking an eye.

I sighed as the elevator rose. It had been a long day. Max and I had helped out with the campus blood drive. Gage had laughed when I'd told him about the drive, but he'd suddenly got very serious.

"You're not donating blood yourself, are you?"

"No," I'd said. He'd seemed satisfied.

"Good, you give me too much as it is. You can't spare any."

I'd rolled my eyes at that, but in the end I had ended up donating. The local hospitals were in need as the campus vampire (not Gage), had put a half dozen people into intensive care. Between that and the regular amount of accidents and emergencies, they needed a lot of blood at the moment.

That's why I'd grabbed myself a snack, even though Gage was certain to feed me dinner. I'd grabbed myself a twelve inch sandwich with turkey, swiss and bacon to try and replace what I'd lost, but I there was no hiding what I'd done from him. He'd notice the tiny puncture wound, even if I took off the gauze. He'd be annoyed.

And that was why I'd bought the brown sugar tea with pudding and cream foam that he liked. For myself, I had taro milk tea with tapioca pearls, because I was determined to work my way through the entire menu. I couldn't wait to try it.

Gage waited at the door to his apartment, and I could feel the smallest frisson of excitement in my stomach from him, the empathic link from our bond transmitting his feelings to me. It was nice to feel wanted, and I was sure he could feel my own trepidation alongside my joy to see him. The trepidation and even the joy were quickly replaced by something else.

Gage leaned on his front door frame wearing nothing but black boxer briefs. I almost dropped everything I was carrying, focused on the hard planes of his slim body, the muscles of his chest and abs. My mouth went dry then rapidly filled with saliva. Like Pavlov's dog I was salivating just from the sight of him.

"Come here, Puppy, don't just stand there in the hall with your mouth open."

I hadn't realized I'd stopped moving. Without a second thought I obeyed. Making my big, heavy feet move one after the other took conscious effort. Gage, when he was all sleek and predatory like this, made me feel awkward. Too tall, all elbows and knees and unsure of myself.

And I loved that.

I hadn't expected to, and I didn't want to think too deeply as to why I craved feeling awkward and out of control. Instead I gave in, because Gage was hot and he was more than willing to give me what I needed. I could trust him to give me what I needed. He'd make me feel small in the best possible way.

I pressed the brown sugar milk tea into his hands, kissed him on the cheek then sat at the table with my dinner. I got more nervous, sure he was about to notice the pinprick on my elbow where the blood had been withdrawn.

Gage moved close behind me, caressing the back of my neck and humming. "Why are you nervous, Puppy? I can feel it."

I swallowed. "Uh..." I picked up my sandwich and took a bite, wildly hoping that he'd somehow forget he asked if I took long enough to chew and swallow.

Gage's fingers adjusted, gripping the back of my neck.

"Answer the question, Brand."

I swallowed my mouthful and reached up to touch his forearm. "You're gonna be angry."

"Tell me." His grip intensified.

Arousal shot through me despite the nervousness.

"I gave blood at the blood drive, even though you didn't want me to."

He let go of my neck and kissed the top of my head.

"Good boy for telling me." He moved around to sit opposite me at the table, sipping his bubble tea. "This is good."

I relaxed, but only slightly. I didn't like keeping things from Gage. On top of that, I was certain he was going to punish me. We hadn't done much punishment. He'd said he would save it for when I was more used to submitting, back when we'd first agreed to be partners. But that had been weeks ago now.

He watched me, eyes sharp, as I ate my sandwich.

"You're going to punish me, aren't you?" I asked, after we'd been sitting in relative silence for a time. Just asking it out loud I was sporting a half-chub. I'm sure he could detect that arousal on me, as well as everything else.

His eyes darkened, and he set the now empty cup down on the table soundlessly.

"Do you think you deserve punishment?"

"I..." I swallowed. "Yes. I disobeyed you."

"You did." He shifted, placing one elbow on the table and resting his chin in his hand. "Eat up, pup."

I finished eating as fast as I could, and gulped down the taro tea.

Gage watched, one eyebrow artfully raised, barely moving.

Once I was done and had wiped my mouth and tidied away the wrapper, Gage stood and pointed at the bedroom. "In there, naked and kneeling, pet."

I went straight in, my heart thumping with anticipation.

4

BRANDON

I got naked and knelt as quickly as I could, excited for what would happen, but the door to the bedroom remained closed. Gage made me wait.

This was probably the torture, I thought.

He wanted to test how patient I was.

Well, I could be patient. I'd show him just how good and obedient I could be.

I took a deep breath and listened. No sound.

Vampires don't have to make sound if they didn't want to. He'd just displayed that with his cup on the table.

Sweat beaded on my forehead. I *hated* waiting. Gage could probably tell, with the empathy link. He was probably laughing, feeling my impatience.

Finally, I heard the swish of the door open.

I listened hard for where he was in the room but he walked silently as a cat.

Gage gripped my shoulder.

I startled, not expecting it.

His voice was low in my ear. "Pet, this is your first time being punished, so I want you to know that if it's too much you can safeword, all right?"

"Yes, sir."

"Tell me your safeword again."

My mind went blank and I opened my mouth to say nothing at all. But then I remembered our first night together, how he made me tell him about that Hallowe'en with the pirate.

"Seasalt."

"Good boy. Now. I'm going to blindfold you."

Goosebumps pricked my skin. "Yes sir." Before I could take a breath something silky was tied over my eyes. Firm and secure, it made me hot all over again. Having something taken away. God, I was so *easy* for him. It was like he'd been designed to hit every single hot button I had and wasn't aware of.

"Can you see anything?"

I'd closed my eyes when the silk hit them but now I opened them, trying to see. Gage had done his job well, nothing but darkness. "No sir."

"Good."

His cold fingers ran over my biceps, pulling my arms behind me. He wrapped the sturdy leather cuffs around my wrists and with a *snick* they were locked together. I resisted the urge to tug against them, test my limits, tease myself. I wanted to impress him with how well behaved I could be.

For a long minute nothing more happened and I was once again left to wonder if waiting was going to be the punishment? I couldn't hear Gage moving. I couldn't feel him close by, although I knew he must be.

"Stand."

I swallowed, rocking back on my heels and standing slowly. It was harder than it should have been with my hands bound. I managed it.

The next moment, Gage had his iron grip on my bicep. I was pushed down over the bed, face first. I gasped, squirming to get into the most comfortable position. Gage manhandled me up the bed, pulling a pillow under my hips so my ass was in the air.

"I'm going to spank you but not with my hand, with a paddle." His voice wasn't just a promise, it was smug, full of wicked delight.

I moaned into the bedclothes. I had dreamed about this, but he'd never actually done it. Just how much of a punishment would this be, if I longed for it? I wasn't going to argue with him now. I swallowed hard.

"Count them," he ordered.

I was about to agree when the paddle landed on my left ass cheek. He hadn't done a playful pat. No, this was a solid smack with a stinging aftertaste. The paddle covered more surface area than his hand did. A whole different experience.

"One!" I gasped, moaning as my body translated the sting into heat that pumped straight to my dick.

He brought it down again, this time on the other ass cheek.

"Two." I choked the word out. My body reacted in two opposite ways. It wanted more and it wanted to escape. Staying still for the punishment took all of my strength.

He spanked me twice more in quick succession.

I leaked precum onto the bed as I counted. My voice broke on the word four.

"How many can you take?" Gage's voice sounded cool, detached. His hand gently smoothed over my lower back in a reassuring way.

Checking in, and also asking for my genuine input. My first impulse was to say just five, only get one more and then he'd be fucking me. But I wanted to impress him, and that desire hadn't gone away. My competitive side reared up. I was on the brink of telling him I could take anything, do whatever he wanted. Some calm, rational part of me took over my tongue and split the difference.

"Ten."

Gage's fingers caressed my spanked skin. His touch was gentle but I recoiled with a hiss. I was tender there!

"Such a good boy. Want to impress me, don't you? I can feel it. I can also feel how very hot you are from being corrected like this." He stopped caressing me and I whimpered, missing his touch instantly, aching for it. "Very well. Ten it is."

"Th-thank you, sir."

He spanked me again with the unforgiving paddle. I hadn't thought it had been so bad to start with but it felt intense now.

The pain of each blow felt like a bright spark that died off quickly into arousal, then lit up again with the next impact.

My mind swirled with the sparks, barely keeping me grounded on the bed. Through the sensations I could feel Gage's arousal building as well, he loved how I was reacting to it all.

I think I managed to continue to count.

Gage didn't tell me off so I must have, but my mind wasn't on the numbers, it was swimming in pleasure and pain.

My skin, and my soul lit up like a supernova with each new blow. I was writhing, rutting against the sheets mindlessly, although with no intention to get off just because I had to Do *something*.

"You're a good dog, aren't you? A good puppy for me. Open up."

Gage's fingers tapped my chin and I opened my mouth without thinking. My mind was focused on only two things. The first was doing whatever Gage said, pleasing him with my obedience. The other was maximizing the pleasure I got from him. I felt awash with desire and urgent with need. My dick throbbed, and every chafe against the sheets made my balls tighten, but I knew I had to hold back. If I came before I was given permission, I'd be punished all over again and he might not make it quite so pleasurable.

He slid the leather paddle between my teeth. "Bite down."

I bit. The paddle formed a large bit in my mouth, the kind you might put on a horse. Unbidden, images I'd found online of pony submissives flashed in my head. All that leather, so confining. God was I into that *too?*

I didn't have time for an existential kink crisis. The cold drip of lube on my hole brought me back to the here and now.

Gage's fingers were rough, stretching and pulling at me as if he couldn't wait to get inside me. I didn't care. I was ready for him and I didn't care how much it hurt. I tried to tell him this but with my teeth clamped shut it mostly came out as a needy moan.

"Quiet pet, you'll get what I give you."

Well, I could hardly argue with that. I relaxed as best I could into the rough treatment, reasoning that if it was quicker to prep me then it was sooner that I got fucked.

The blindfold heightened everything he did. I was aware of his thighs, pushing my own apart. Every inch that our skin touched felt electric.

He stretched the tight ring of muscle, using two or three fingers now, I was so lost in the sensations my body was feeling I could hardly tell. His fingers were my main focus but I was still stinging from the paddle.

Finally, he withdrew his fingers and lined himself up.

"Please," I moaned, through the paddle in my mouth.

"Good boy." His hand ruffled my hair and then his fingers gripped tight, yanking my head up.

He pushed inside. My body quickly adjusted to the feeling of fullness that came from his dick. I breathed out heavily. The relief of actually being fucked after the punishment was so great my eyes watered. I was grateful for the blindfold then, as it soaked up the tears.

"You like that, do you? Tell me how much you like being filled with your master's dick."

I tried to speak around the paddle but the words came out garbled. But the 'yes' was relatively clear.

25

Gage grunted, his hand twisting in my hair to give me a flash of pain in my scalp. I groaned, loving every second.

Then he started to pound me.

The smacking of skin on skin filled the room, soon drowned out by my moans. With each thrust he smacked into my inflamed ass cheeks, adding a new dimension to the sensations.

My jaw ached from clenching my teeth on the leather paddle but I didn't dare let go of it.

"So good. Such a good, pliant boy, aren't you?" Gage leaned down over my back, releasing my hair to wind his long fingers around my throat instead. "Answer me."

Around the paddle, I grunted "yes, Master"

"Just love to be used like this don't you? You love it when I take away your choices, and make you do what I want."

I screwed my eyes shut under the blindfold. "Mmhmm."

Gage chuckled, a sound that tingled through my blood. I felt the cresting wave of his oncoming orgasm, fed to me by our blood link, and knew he felt just how hot and flustered I was.

He reached around underneath and started to jerk me off.

I tried to hitch my hips up to give him more access but he never stopped pounding me so it was a lost cause. I abandoned the effort and groaned louder.

"Come when I do, puppy. That's my good boy."

It would have been impossible not to. My own arousal was heightened by his, and I could feel his orgasm crashing as surely as if I saw it happening.

I came in the same instant, my mouth going slack as I moaned out the pleasure, riding it like a wave to shore.

Gage pumped a few more times and then pulled out. He tugged off the blindfold, unlocked the cuffs and clean me up, but all I could do was lie there and try to catch my ragged breath.

He pulled me into his arms as I recovered.

Finally, my head cleared enough to realize something. "You didn't feed."

"You already gave blood today." Gage huffed, not meeting my eyes. "I don't want you getting faint."

I smilee. Such a mean and demanding Master, but my vampire boyfriend was a sweetheart really.

5

BRANDON

I woke up wrapped in soft as satin sheets and content in the knowledge that Gage was close by. He wasn't in bed with me. He was in the next room over. The connection between us was almost physically palpable, a scarlet thread that was always present, but not always as strong as it was now.

Yawning, I rolled over to check the time and swore. I scrambled out of bed, almost falling over as my limbs got tangled. I had to boost if I was going to make it to my classes in time.

I took a shower, enjoying how quickly I could clean under the monsoon shower head, dried off in record time, dressed and hurried out. I paused in the living room, looking for where I'd dropped my backpack the night before.

Gage poked his head out from his office. "Do you want breakfast?"

"No time!"

But I made time to go back and kiss him goodbye.

After the kiss, he tutted. "There's protein bars in the pantry, at least take a couple of those with you."

I chuckled. He looked like a punk goth kid but he fussed like a grandpa. A wave of affection warmed my chest.

"Fine, I will."

He pinched my ass as I turned away. "See you soon. Text me." He went back to work.

I grabbed a handful of protein bars and made my way out of the building.

It was a bright day. Sunshine was always dazzling after the intentional gloom of Gage's apartment. I demolished a peanut butter bar and one blueberry oat. I slid into the back of the lecture theater just as the professor started talking.

At lunch time I met up with Max and we ate sandwiches from the new food cart.

"Nice to see you, stranger."

I shoved his shoulder, playfully. "Shut up. I'm doing the thing you wanted me to do and seeing the same person in a monogamous way. You don't get to complain about it now."

Max laughed and shoved me back. "I can complain all I want."

"Jerk."

He stuck his tongue out at me like we were fourteen again. "Jackass."

───

That afternoon, I spent an hour in the library finding references for a paper, and then went to my last class of the day. It was a two-hour affair that even the professor seemed bored by. I made notes now and then but inevitably my mind began to drift.

What was also inevitable was *where* my mind drifted to.

Gage.

It was impossible *not* to think of him when my ass still smarted from the spanking he'd given me. I relived it in vivid detail. How hot had it been to be corrected? The humiliation aspect hit something in me that had never been satisfied with any of my other lovers.

It was strange because Gage was shorter than me. The times I'd looked up BDSM porn, gay por, or any kind really, the bigger guy was always on top. The bigger guy had the power. But Gage, even though he was shorter, slighter than me in every way, he was so much stronger.

Control practically leaked from his pores, and he wore it like a badge of honor.

He loved it.

And I loved it too. I wanted to give everything to him — but the idea of *everything*. That scared me a bit. I wanted to be with him 24/7, couldn't stop thinking about him. But I wanted to finish school as well. To graduate, get a diploma and a job. I wanted to see whales up close someday. Travel to the Great Barrier Reef. Maybe even visit Antarctica for the penguins.

I couldn't imagine Gage on a research vessel, not for a moment.

It would be so easy to let go of all those desires, the small amount of ambition I had, throw it all over and just belong to Gage.

The idea of it was tempting, more tempting than felt healthy, given how short a time we'd known each other. But the way he talked, the stuff about soulmates... It felt so real, so true to me.

I imagined myself arriving at his place with my bags, my surfboard under one arm. Just telling him "I'm yours. This is it, do what you want from now until eternity."

He'd love it.

I could picture it so clearly.

Gage would start by stripping me off. Then he'd wrap me in leather straps, all of them buckled tight. Thighs, ankles, wrists, biceps, criss-crossing my torso and of course a heavy one around my neck. He'd padlock them, toss away the keys so even if I wanted to, I couldn't get them off. I'd be his.

He'd force me to my knees. Look down on me with that intensity, that hunger, and that absolute self-satisfaction reveling in his ultimate control. My pants were getting tight thinking about it.

He'd make me suck him off, for sure. Kneeling on the floor at his feet. Then he'd yank me up, chain me to the bed and fuck me raw, bite me and drink his fill of my blood.

Fuck. I was getting semi-hard, and I was still in class.

I pulled my hoody over my lap and took a deep drink from my water bottle. I couldn't get hard in class, I had to focus.

But my imagination was taken with the scenario I'd come up with. Although I tried my best to pay attention to the slides, my mind wandered right back to Gage.

I imagined his cool hand caressing my skin, teasing... He was always teasing, making me whine and ultimately beg for him to do more. Beg for him to fuck me, and to let me come.

My phone buzzed.

Gage: R U THINKING ABOUT ME

I blushed as if he could see me. He couldn't see me.

But the blood tether between us must be strong enough that he could feel me. Feel me getting horny as hell when I was literally in class.

I swallowed, and thumbed a reply.

Brand: no
Gage: Liar
Gage: I can feel you
Gage: feels good, why aren't you here?
Brand: okay fine I was thinking about you
Gage: i knew it
Gage: getting hot for me
Gage: Where are you?
Brand: in class
Gage: naughty boy
Gage: getting hot for me on campus

```
Brand: shut up
Gage: Don't think so. Im not supposed to be
concentrating on class I can do whatever
I want
        Gage: You're so hot I can feel it from here
        Gage: tell me what you're thinking about
```

Gage was making it a whole thing. Sweat beaded on my
forehead. He'd taken to texting me like this. One message after
the other, as if the send button was an enter key. He was
relentless. I should shut it down, concentrate on my course. I
gave it a half-hearted try.

```
Brand: I have class
    Gage: idc tell me
    Gage: in detail
    Gage: give specifics
```

Fuck

I started texting him. Thumbs moving quick as I could
manage. I left out the context of moving in but went into detail
about the straps and the padlocks. I'd seen stuff online with
locking mechanisms and padlocks and it always made me
squirm. I typed it all out and sent it in one big message. I sat
there, breathless, aware I must be bright red around the face. I
glanced around me but none of the other students had noticed.
Thank goodness.

He didn't reply right away, letting me stew in my own
thoughts and arousal. It was torture. Being made to wait again.
Being made to wait when I'd just spilled a risque fantasy to my
smoking hot boyfriend via text message.

I hated how he did this, but I loved it too.

Finally, when I was crossing my legs and trying to think of something deeply unsexy, he replied.

```
Gage: good boy
    Gage: how hard are you?
    Brand: exceptionally. Granite has nothing
on me. Steel wishes it could
    Gage: wanna cum?
```

I barely stifled a groan. Of course I wanted to come, but I was literally in class. Surrounded by people. I wasn't exactly a quiet person. There was no way I could. But I wanted to.

```
Brand: I'm in class
    Gage: next time you pass a restroom go in
    Gage: go into a stall and lock the door
    Gage: text me
```

I breathed out, somewhat relieved.

```
Brand: k
    Gage: good puppy
```

The rest of the class passed so slowly I was afraid I might pass out.

I could have tried to leave, just run to the nearest restroom and call Gage, demanding he talk me through it.

But there were three problems with that plan.

First, I'd have to squeeze past other students just to get to the aisle, and I was sporting a hardon that would be impossible to hide at close quarters.

Two, I'd risk missing the professor announcing an upcoming quiz, or assignment or something. He always left those to the last five minutes of the class.

Thirdly, Gage would know that I'd skipped out on my class, and he'd tell me off, and maybe even punish me. Even though he was the one encouraging this... whatever it was, I still wanted to be good for him.

Slowly my dick calmed down, although not all the way it wasn't as painfully stiff any more. I concentrates enough to make a couple of notes. True to my suspicions, our professor talked about the next assignment and told us to start thinking of topics now, so we could start to gather materials.

Finally, finally everyone was getting up and shuffling slowly out of the room.

I made my way into the corridor. There was a restroom a floor down, but I was also pretty sure there was one in the basement level, and that one would absolutely be the quietest available. A few more minutes couldn't hurt.

I took the stairs down to the basement two at a time, heart pounding as I imagined what Gage might say to me, how he was going to make me come remotely.

I opened the door to the men's room and as I'd expected, it was totally empty. I hurried to the first stall, locked myself in and hung my bag from the hook on the back of the door. I pulled my phone out, leaning against the stall wall.

Brand: I'm in the men's room
 Gage: good boy
 Gage: took you long enough

That felt like bait so I didn't take it, for once I was the patient one.

Gage: you don't feel as hot now
    Gage: read through what you sent me, and imagine it happening
    Gage: because it's going to happen
    Gage: i promise

My dick stood to attention. I did what he said, reading through my message, picturing it just as I had the first time. This time it had a better edge to it, because Gage had promised it would happen. Now it wasn't just a fantasy, I had it to look forward to.

I imagined Gage feeling my horniness remotely, how satisfied and smug he was about getting me like this. Me giving him this access to my fantasies and then acting on them. My breathing was ragged.

Brand: k, done
    Gage: good boy, now undo your pants and stroke yourself through your underwear
    Gage: text me so I know you're doing it

I undid the top button on my jeans and shoved them down over my hips. I palmed myself and stroked myself, wrapping the fabric of my boxers around my dick to give it some friction. With my left hand I typed my reply.

. . .

```
Brand: doing it
   Gage: good boy
   Gage: stroke long and slow
   Gage: how does it feel?
Brand: gd
Brand: good
   Gage: now, spit on your hand and pull
yourself out
```

I obeyed as quickly as possible. I didn't want to stop touching myself now that I'd started, I wanted more. I quickly replied, bracing my phone against my jeans.

```
Brand: done
   Gage: quicker now pet
   Gage: imagine it's me touching you
   Gage: I'm behind you, breathing down your
sexy neck, one hand on your throat, the other
stroking you
   Gage: you like that?
   Gage: I'd have you bound up, cuffs locked
like you want, can't get away, can't do
anything but take what I give you
```

I stifled a needy moan. There was no one else in the restroom, right? I could probably be loud. I pressed my forehead into the stall wall, relishing the coolness against my hot skin. I had to reply to him.

```
Brand: fcuk yeah feels good
```

```
Gage: yeah it does
Gage: my little pet, my fuck toy
Gage: your pleasure is mine
Gage: and it feels good, you're so horny
aren't you? Bet you're sweating hard
Gage: I could withhold it if I wanted to
Gage: if I didn't tell you to cum you
wouldn't, would you?
```

I whined, terrified that he'd do just that, withhold it. He'd know if I came, he could feel how hot I was. I'd have to stay aroused. Thankfully that had been my last class of the day, so I could head to Gage's right after if I had to. But in this state?

```
Brand: please don't
Gage: answer me
Gage: you'd stop if I told you to, right?
```

I swallowed hard, but I knew the truth as much as he did.

```
Brand: yeah, I'd stop
Gage: good boy
Gage: get yourself off
Gage: I want to feel you cum from here,
knowing that if I'd said no, you wouldn't have
done it
```

Thank fuck. I tightened my fist and stroked myself, getting myself off as quickly as I could. It was rough, too dry for my liking even with the generous amount of precum I was leaking, but it didn't matter. I was so aroused, I came hard, staring at the words on my phone screen, imagining Gage there with me.

I mopped up with some toilet roll and took a moment to catch my breath.

```
Gage: that's my good boy
   Gage: proud of you
   Gage: text me a selfie, right now
```

I picked up my phone and snapped a shot of myself. I looked wrecked. Face shiny with sweat, hair mussed, I must have been tossing my head. My eyes were wide, pupils blown and cheeks bright red. I looked as if I'd just come in a public restroom. I sent it to him.

```
Gage: hot, saving that one
   Gage: see you later?
```

Just like that he was back to a normal conversation. Had he come as well? I hadn't sensed anything but then my own arousal had been nearly overwhelming.

```
Brand: yeah, gonna grab some clothes and
things from home then I'll come around
   Gage: I'll order you in pizza when you
get here
```

What a bizarre thing to say, thanking him for pizza but not for the stupendous orgasm he'd just given me. Well, maybe it would count for both.

I cleaned myself up as best I could, splashed my face with cold water at the basin and dried off with a paper towel. Had I just done that? Got myself so worked up that Gage would feel it, and that he'd control me remotely just via text.

It felt unreal.

I looked at myself in the mirror, and decided I looked normal enough to leave the restroom. Grabbing my bag from the stall, I tried to get my thoughts back in order. What was I supposed to be doing?

I walked through the hallways and out into the fresh air. Somehow, the sun was still shining. I felt like it should be night at the very least.

But it wasn't, and Gage wasn't expecting me for a while yet.

Leaving campus, I stopped off at a coffee shop to grab something to perk me up.

It was a busy time of day, three lines going at once.

Usually, I would have pulled out my phone and played around on it, but I'd left the text chain from Gage up before I locked it and I was worried that if I saw the words again it'd be back to square one, aroused and alone in public.

I shoved my hands in my pockets and read the menu, for something to do.

After a moment I realized someone was watching me. They weren't subtle about it, which helped, but all those nights I'd spent cruising clubs and parties had given me a very sharp awareness for when I was noticed. I glanced to my left. There were two people in the queue next to me.

He was taller than me and lanky, with sharp features and a

straight, slightly upturned nose. He had dark blond hair and his startling blue eyes were taking me in like he wanted to take me home. Beside him was a slighter woman, petite with her hair combed out into full puffs. Her eyes were a deep brown, checking me out in a more subtle way.

I looked away, hoping they'd get the hint.

"Hey there." The man's voice was deep, resonant. "What's your name, cutie?"

I looked back.

Matching smiles greeted me. No hints had been got.

A month ago, before I'd met Gage, I probably would have flirted with them. But that was a month ago, and now I was in a very different situation.

"Not interested," I said in a friendly way. Thankfully my queue moved, and I stepped forward. Something about the pair unsettled me. Who comes onto someone for a threeway waiting in line for coffee? At least wait until you've ordered, and no one has anything to do but wait for their name to be called. Hopefully they wouldn't continue the conversation.

Their line moved up too, and they were beside me again.

The man extended a hand. "Perhaps you'd prefer to give us your name after learning ours first? I'm Ford, and this is Shawna. We'd both very much like to get to know you better."

I ignored the outstretched hand and shook my head. "That's really nice and all but I'm just here for a coffee."

The next instant, Shawna moved closer to me, reaching for the pendant around my neck, the wolf crest that Gage had given me. "What a beautiful necklace. Does it mean something? To you? Perhaps it's of spiritual significance?"

I moved a half step back so she couldn't touch it. The idea of her being in personal space raised the hairs on the back of my neck. "Yeah, my boyfriend gave it to me. Boyfriend, you know? So you see why I'm not interested in the two of you, yeah?"

Shawna leaned closer in, although she didn't touch me. "Oh, you'll be very interested in us, Brandon. Just you wait."

I swallowed hard.

I hadn't told them my name.

I didn't know what to say, so I just stared at her. My stomach roiled.

What would Gage do if he felt my fear? I wasn't in any actual danger, so I took a deep breath to calm myself down.

"Ah, look at you. You're delicious, so responsive." Her face broke into a beautiful smile, the kind of smile poets write about, dawn breaking and all of that. She looked away. "Come along, Ford, I know when we're not wanted."

She took his hand and they both swept out of the shop as if it was a turn of the century ballroom.

I swallowed again. The person who'd been standing behind them in line moved forward, their headphones still on, eyes locked on their phone. I glanced around to see if anyone else had noticed that weird exchange, but it seemed no one had. It was as if I'd imagined it.

"Next, please!"

I stepped up to the counter to make my order.

6

BRANDON

I found the apartment empty. Max had stuck a note on the fridge door telling me to text more often. I took a picture of it and sent it to him, chuckling at my own wit.

With no one to talk to, and nothing that needed doing at home, I packed a few changes of clothes, the rest of my school binders and notebooks into a duffel and headed out again.

It was close to what I'd fantasized about, arriving at Gage's with bags of stuff, but the fact was I was thinking more and more of just making his place my more permanent abode.

It made a lot of sense, especially since he'd been as good as his word and had started buying me things more often.

When were we going to go suit shopping? Gage kept talking about it but we never actually went.

I imagined him outfitting me in a suit, and then in various other get ups...

"Come on, Brand, stay chill. Don't want him feeling you get all horny again."

I thought about my school assignment as I walked over to Gage's, bag over my shoulder. That was a good, safe topic that wouldn't cause any accidental arousal.

Gage met me at the door, no doubt sensing as I got close. I sensed him too, a silvery beacon that got stronger as I neared it.

"Hey, it's my favorite lighthouse." I leaned in to kiss him.

"Lighthouse? That's a new one." He kissed me back and drew me in by the waist. His apartment smelled of hot cheese and pepperoni. My stomach rumbled.

"Yeah, because I can sense you from far away."

"And I keep you safe?"

"That too." I dropped my bag on the floor and made my way to the pizza boxes on the kitchen table.

"By all means, help yourself." Gage was amused.

I flashed him a grin as I sat and pulled the top box towards me, taking a slice. "Thanks. You're the best."

Gage went to the fridge and came back with two bottles of vegetable juice. He opened one and set it beside me. "Gotta keep your vitamins up. I know your metabolism won't care about all this grease, but it's in my best interests to keep you healthy."

"You think of everything." I spoke through a mouthful of pizza.

He winced.

"Well, with a boyfriend as charming as you are, how could I not?"

"Your sarcasm is noted."

I finished off half the pizza in record time as Gage asked about my classes and told me about his day buying and selling online.

"Then of course, I felt something through the connection, and well. You know how that went."

I beamed. "Yeah I do."

"So. What do you feel like doing tonight? After this afternoon I'm not sure how creative I can be." Gage stretched his arms over his head.

He seemed tired.

I wasn't sure exactly how vampires rested, he never seemed to sleep, but they must need to do *something* right?

I wanted to give him a break, to encourage him to rest and take care of himself. And like he said, we'd had an intense session remotely that afternoon. A quiet evening might be just the thing for both of us. It almost felt taboo to suggest such a thing, it was so different to how we usually spent our time together, but I had to be honest about how much energy I had as well.

"I reckon," I said, slowly. "I finish up another slice of pizza, and we move to the couch and watch a movie."

Gage's eyebrows shot up. "A movie?"

"Yeah, they're these modern things with moving pictures and music," I said.

"You asshole, I know what movies are." He kicked me under the table.

"You're a vampire, I don't know how up to date you are on modern technology."

"I was turned in the fucking eighties, and I spend all day on my computer." Gage stood up and shook his head. "If you start making old person jokes I swear I'll—"

"Okay, okay." I held up my hands in surrender. "I just thought it'd be fun, something different for us. Maybe we could have ice cream and snacks?"

Gage's expression softened. "You really want to just sit and watch movies?"

I licked my lips. "Well, I maybe want to cuddle too."

"You got it." Gage looked relieved.

I was glad I'd put it out there. I loved fucking him, and all the weird, kinky shit he introduced me to, but tonight I just wanted to have a boyfriend.

We settled on the couch, Gage pulled a soft, furry blanket from a box I'd never noticed before in the living area, and handed me the remote as he settled it over us. I flicked on the TV.

His TV was the biggest I'd ever seen outside a shop. It was weird to think I'd never actually seen it switched on. He had every streaming service available, plus cable, all collected as apps to select from.

I went looking for *Point Break*, one of my favorites of all time, and soon had it selected.

"You seen this before?"

Gage shook his head. "I dunno I just never really clicked with Keanu."

"You really are a monster. Well, we're watching this and then some other righteous movies featuring my main man." I hit play.

Gage slipped his arm around me. "I thought *I* was your main man."

He put on a ridiculous, over-exaggerated pout. His lower lip stuck out like a child's.

I smirked.

"I'm sorry, but no one comes close to Mr Reeves. You'll just have to get used to being second best."

Gage started ruthlessly tickling me, and I was forced to pause the movie.

7

BRANDON

The next day was Saturday. When I woke up I was in no mood to study so I went looking for Gage. He was at his computer looking stressed. I slung my arms over his shoulders and rested my chin on top of his head.

"Good morning." His voice was dry as old paper. "I'm guessing you want attention." I laughed. "Yeah, but I also want to do something. Can you go out in the daytime?"

Gage shifted, uncrossing his legs. "Yeah, I just shouldn't do it too often. Where are you thinking?"

"Maybe you could take me shopping like you keep on suggesting?"

Gage perked up so much he shrugged me off him. His chair spun and he looked up at me, impossibly eager. "Really?"

"Yeah, why not? You want to spoil me, I want to go out..."

"Perfect. Okay, we'll hit up Gucci first and then just make our way through the fashion district."

He stood up. Suddenly his face was a mere inch from my face. I inhaled.

"And of course, the finest leatherworker around."

I leaned in and kissed him before he could comment on how red my cheeks went at the mention of a leatherworker.

Twenty minutes later we were downtown in the fashion district. Gage had pulled on a baseball cap and large dark sunglasses. He looked like a movie star trying to stay incognito. I slipped my arm through his and felt like the king of the world, out with my steady boyfriend who was also the hottest vampire ever to live. Was live the right word? Exist, maybe?

"Here, let's get you measured." Gage tugged me into the Gucci store.

I'd walked past a thousand times but never gone in. I had a horror of walking in, touching something and it immediately breaking, forcing me to pay for it. I held my breath as Gage ushered me in first.

I'd never got a firm understanding of just how much cash he had, but I had the notion it was in the millions if not billions.

The shop interior was more like a museum than a store. Stark white surfaces, targeted lighting, and huge photographs of beautiful famous people I didn't recognize wearing Gucci.

Gage went straight up to the first service person.

The young woman with a perfectly made up face smiled politely, no doubt having already taken in my rather battered clothing and Gage's understated, yet expensive outfit.

"Good morning. How can I help?"

"I'd like to get my boyfriend here measured for a suit. We'll pick the style after."

"Absolutely, come right this way."

She led me to the back of the store where there was a huge changing room, sectioned off with a black curtain.

A man with a British accent took over from her. "Please stand on this dais, and I'll take your measurements, sir."

I did as he said, holding my arms up as directed.

Gage sat in a velvet armchair and watched, sunglasses dangling idly from his hand. He looked utterly at home. I felt awkward, too tall, out of place. Sure I was about to say or do something that was a dreadful faux pas.

The man made notes on an iPad as he worked. The most awkward moment was when he took my leg inseam measurement. It felt rather too intimate. Gage's face went carefully blank.

"I'm finished, unless you wish to be measured for a hat?"

"No, thanks." I stepped down off the box and pulled my T-shirt back on. Gage stood, grabbed my waist and pulled me in for a kiss.

"Mine."

"You can't seriously be jealous of a tailor who you told to measure me?" I whispered, pleased beyond reason.

"I don't like people touching my things."

I pressed against him for two seconds, and then pulled away. I fluttered my eyelashes at him. "So, what kind of suit?"

Gage eyed me.

I knew I hadn't gotten away with playing innocent about teasing him like that. That was fine. If I could rile him up during the shopping trip I'd have a lot of fun later in the day. I might even get punished again.

Wanting to be punished was new. If you'd told me I'd be into it six months ago, I'd have laughed.

Gage gave me a dark look full of promise, and then we were into the serious business of choosing a style.

Shopping wasn't something I could do for hours on end. I liked the idea, and touching pretty things and trying things on, but Gage was intense about it. He picked out shoes, three suits including a tuxedo, accessories, and even designer socks. I was almost yawning when he finally paid for it all, and gave them his address for the suits to be delivered to when they were done.

He took my hand as we left the store. We had no bags to carry. Apparently clothing delivery was something rich people just did.

"That was a lot of money," I said.

"Yep, and you're gonna look incredible." He looked up at me as he slipped his sunglasses on. "You pick the next place."

I looked around for something more my style. "There, Superdry."

Gage chuckled. "Of course, surfer boy."

I had more fun in that shop, picking out T-shirts and tanks in multiple colors and designs, a few hoodies. I eyed jeans but Gage shook his head.

"We can get you a better cut than this." He paid and I took the bulging shopping bags.

As we headed into the sunlight, Gage paused to stick his sunglasses on. I looked around at the crowd, not really thinking anything until I recognized a face. The weird woman from the coffee place the other day.

I narrowed my eyes.

She also wore sunglasses, and didn't appear to have noticed me. She moved through the press of people fluidly, never touching anyone and never breaking her stride.

My blood ran cold, seeing her again. It occurred to me that I'd never mentioned the unsettling encounter to Gage. I probably should have.

"You okay? You look weird and feel weirder."

I glanced at him. "Yeah, I just saw..." I looked back. She was gone. I turned to the direction she had been moving — nothing. "I just saw someone. This weird thing happened at the coffee shop near campus the other day and I think it was her."

Gage frowned and scanned the crowd, then looked up at me. "What happened?"

"Just, these two people, acting like they wanted to pick me up or something and then they knew my name?"

"Had they just heard it called out when you got your coffee?"

"No, it was before I ordered." I chewed on my lip, looking all

49

around. My heart racing like at any moment I was going to be pounced on, and not in a fun way.

Someone leaned in a doorway, talking on the phone. The long lanky guy.

I grabbed Gage's arm. "There, by that boarded up green door. That guy."

Gage slipped his arm around my waist and followed the direction of my gaze. "Huh."

"Huh?"

Gage gripped my arm and walked briskly in the other direction, off the main drag and back towards where he'd parked his car.

"Vampire."

I swallowed. The reason they'd been interested in me became a lot clearer. "Are they like your enemies?"

"They're... Well, they're not my friends. I'm not friends with any vampires."

That surprised me. "Really? You don't ever hang out with your own kind?"

Gage unlocked the car and held the door for me. I got in, piling the bags on my feet. He slammed the door and got in on the other side. He only responded once we were driving and had put a bit of distance behind us.

"I live alone and I like it that way. The guy who turned me was a total asshole. Left me to fend for myself. It put me off all the others. Every now and then someone pops up trying to be friends or invite me to a vampire get together, but I always send them packing."

His grip on the steering wheel was tight.

How should I approach this? I was desperately curious but I didn't want to piss him off further.

"You don't talk about the past much, about how you were turned."

Gage glanced at me and laughed, an ugly, harsh sound.

"Because it's a shit-ass story. You know me now, that's way better."

I put a hand on his knee, unsure if that was something he'd enjoy or if I was pushing things. "Still, it's your past. If you want to talk about it, you can."

Gage grunted, focusing on the road, making turns and finally pulling into the parking lot of a small, run down two-storey building that looked abandoned except for a sign hanging over the door.

"Listen, I know you mean well, but like I said, it's a shit story. Depressing. Let's just leave it at I don't hang with other vampires, okay?"

"Yeah, that's cool."

He put the car into park and lifted my hand from his knee, gently kissing my knuckles.

"You gotta let me know if you ever see them again, though, right?"

"Right." I smiled at him, feeling watery somehow. Like I was about to plunge through thin ice into a freezing river. At least he wasn't mad at me for not telling him about the earlier encounter.

"Now, where the hell have you brought me?"

Gage's tense expression lit up into a wide smile with a devilish spark in his eye. "*Montague's.*"

8

BRANDON

Montague's, it turned out, looked horribly run down on the outside because the owner liked it that way.

"But, don't you miss out on customers? You're so out of the way." I looked around. We were in the front room, which had a small red loveseat, a vintage desk and a velvet curtain.

The owner, who Gage introduced me to as Sir Montague, shook my hand and smiled coldly. He was shorter than me and wore a pristine Oxford shirt, a tailored brown waistcoat and matching suit pants. He had brown hair, styled in a perfect quiff. Something about him made my hackles rise. He wasn't human, like me, but it was possible he was a vampire.

But Gage had just said he didn't like other vampires, so maybe he wasn't that either?

"I would prefer only a certain sort of clientele come to my store," he said. "Such as your friend, Gage here."

"Boyfriend." Gage stuck his hands in his pockets, looking away. "Brand is my boyfriend."

Montague's eyebrows shot up his forehead. "Well now, I've never heard Gage introduce anyone as a boyfriend before. You must be special indeed."

I stood there, uncertain of what to say and vaguely blushing. "I...Thanks?"

"So, what will you be needing today?"

Gage tapped a finger on his chin. "Harness, cuffs, collar and leash, all matching of course. I'm thinking blue if you have it? He's into the ocean."

"Of course, right this way. I have a lovely range of blues at the moment."

Montague led us into the back room. Shallow shelves lined two walls, displaying beautiful leather bondage cuffs of all sizes and colors, collars, and other leather goods. One wall was devoted to saddles, muzzles, and more complex harnesses, hung on their own special hooks to show them off to best advantage. I felt a semi-chub seeing the puppy hoods, kitten ears and pony headpieces, complete with metal bits and reins. On the final wall were railings from which hung all manner of whips, paddles and so on. The middle of the floor was mostly display tables, showing off even more beautiful handmade leather goods, and a large jewelry cabinet devoted to butt plugs, cock rings and nipple clamps. Finally, in one corner there was a clothing rack with leather apparel hanging from it, such as shorts, corsets and bodysuits.

Gage put his hand on the small of my back and pushed me further into the room. "I can feel you getting hot, pet. Ppick out the items that do that the most."

Montague smiled widely. "There's a changing room through the pink door. Call if you need anything and remember, I can custom make almost anything you can imagine."

He moved out of the room, the velvet curtain swishing back into place.

"This is unbelievable."

"Bit better than the sex shops you're used to, eh?"

"I'll say. I hardly know where to start."

Gage's hand on my back directed me to the cuffs section.

"Then let's start here. Look, ocean blue... what do you think?"
He pointed to a set of thick leather cuffs, dyed the color of the
Pacific.

I swallowed, thinking of my recent fantasies. "Do they... Are
they the locking kind?"

Gage picked them up and showed me the extra ring built
into the strap. "They are indeed. Do you want to try them on? I'd
love to lock you into this, baby."

I didn't trust myself to answer with anything but a whimper
or a moan so I nodded and held out my hands to him.

"Good boy." Gage wrapped the supple leather around my
wrist and buckled it tight. "How does it feel?"

I flexed my wrist a few times. "Really comfortable."

"Excellent. Now, is there a matching... yes, look. How do you
like this style of collar?"

It was a sturdy-looking play collar, several layers of leather
fixed together, with a thick D ring in the front. I picked it up and
turned it, finding the little locking mechanism in back. "Can I
try this on too?"

Gage's eyes lit up. "Pass it here, let's try it."

He wrapped it around my neck but didn't fasten it, just
holding it there to check the height. I swallowed, loving the feel
of it, cool and soft, but sturdy.

"Not too tall? Not tall enough?"

"No, it feels good, secure. I like it."

"I'll get Montague to make a puppy tag to hang off the front."
Gage took the collar off me.

I still had the cuff on one wrist so I held it out for him, and
he removed that as well. I immediately missed the feel of it.

"Now, what else? Go look at the clothing, I bet you'd look
incredible in leather booty shorts."

I did as he said, slipping into the pleasant, fuzzy state he
could put me into. Secure in the knowledge that he'd take care
of me wrapping around me like a blanket. I found some shorts

in black leather that looked about my size and pulled them down. Gage adding matching blue items to his pile.

"I'm gonna try these on, okay?" I held the shorts up for Gage to see.

He grinned, showing his fangs. "Good."

In the changing room I took a minute to breathe and calm my heart rate before I stripped off my jeans and shimmied into the leather shorts. It was as if they'd been made for me. They slipped neatly over my hips and when fastened, hugged the curve of my ass. There was even a little extra space in front for my junk. It was a great look for me. My legs looked ten times longer, and my ass utterly spankable.

I went back out into the shop to show them off to Gage, practically bursting with excitement.

He was going through the selection of whips, so I cleared my throat. When he turned to look, he clutched his chest. "Oh fuck it's even better than I imagined. Spin for me."

I was only too happy to. I spun on the spot then cocked my hip, facing away.

In an instant he was pressed against me, his hands on my waist pulling me tight against him.

I gasped, relaxing back into his chest. "I take it you like what you see?"

"I'm gonna eat you alive," he growled in my ear.

His hand trailed up my thigh, chill skin giving me goosebumps as it travelled higher, towards the leather encasing me.

I forgot how to breathe until he let go again. "Go change back, I don't want to be kicked out of Montague's for inappropriate behavior."

I changed back, taking a moment in the changing room to stroke myself - just once, to relieve a bit of the tension. I pulled my jeans back on and took the shorts out to Gagewho had a sizeable pile of merchandise.

"Come on, let's check out and head home."

Were my shorts the reason for the sudden hurry? While I didn't entirely disagree, I wasn't sure I was done in the shop.

"But I didn't see everything yet."

"We'll come back. Soon even, but right now we need to get home." Gage's tone was urgent. I felt his white hot desire through our emotional link. I swallowed.

"Yeah, let's get home."

9

BRANDON

The moment we were in Gage's apartment, he hustled me into the bedroom. "Naked. Now."

"But don't you want me to put the shorts back on?"

Gage groaned like a man tormented. "Yes, but also I need to fuck you... I still have the mental image, it's seared onto my brain."

I stripped.

Gage started pulling things out of the bag, the blue collar and cuffs.

"Get on your knees. I'm gonna collar you, but this time it's the real thing, okay?"

I went straight to my knees. I knew what he meant from my research online. Collaring wasn't just for play, it was almost like an engagement ring to some couples. The collar symbolized the bond between pet and owner, dom and sub.

"Yeah, I'd really like that."

I put my hands on my thighs and looked up, tilting my chin for him.

"When you have this on, you belong to me and you do as I say or there are consequences, you understand?"

"Yes, sir."

"You can still use a safeword, and I'll be checking in on you regularly."

"I understand."

He slipped the collar around my neck. I dropped my chin so he could buckle it more easily.

He tugged it flush against my skin.

"Do you want me to lock it, pet?"

I swallowed. All my fantasies flashed through my mind. My voice cracked as I replied.

"Yeah."

He tugged sharply on the ring of the collar. "Answer me properly."

"Yes, Master. Please lock the collar."

He moved away to pick up a handful of small golden padlocks from the *Montague's* bag.

I closed my eyes as he fitted the lock through the extra loops in the collar, barely suppressing a moan at the sound of it clicking shut.

"Fuck, look at you, pet."

I opened my eyes to look at him as he took a step back.

"I've barely done anything and you're ready to come for me." He palmed himself through his jeans, his eyes raking over my body.

I licked my lips. "Master, all that time at *Montague's*... I got so excited."

He grinned, wasting no time fastening the cuffs around my wrists. He padlocked these as well. My dick pulsed, leaking precum onto my leg. Finally, he clipped the cuffs together and tugged on them. I moaned out loud this time.

"So hot for me. How much do you love this? Being degraded? Bound up like a slave? Being controlled? Answer me, Brand."

I couldn't lie to him, I'd never been able to lie. Besides, he could feel my arousal through the connection. Could feel what could only be described as elation from the simple click of three little padlocks.

"I love it all so much."

"I know." He tugged on the cuffs sharper this time, pulling me in for a kiss that melted my brain. He ravaged my mouth, licking, biting and sucking. When he pulled away I gasped for breath.

"I want you to think about the locks the entire time." He moved, tugging and pushing me so I was on all fours. "I want you to keep your eyes on the locks on those cuffs. Think about what they mean. Even if you wanted to get away from me, you couldn't. Not without the keys, and only I know where they are. You're entirely my prisoner, Brand, and I'm gonna use you."

I groaned. "Yes, master."

He moved behind me to stretch me, working me over with a generous amount of lube. "When I'm done with you, I'm gonna plug you, so I can use you again later. You like the thought of that, puppy?"

I whimpered. "I... yes, I do. I didn't see you pick up a plug, master."

"Oh, I grabbed a few little toys while you were changing into those shorts." He moaned, leaning in to bite the flesh of my ass sharply.

I yelped at the sudden flash of pain.

"Those shorts, babe. They're gonna drive me crazy. The way your ass looks... so round and plump and biteable." He bit me again.

This time I was somewhat prepared. Instead of a yelp I moaned.

"Want to look good for you." He was still fingering me open as I spoke, and my voice was so breathy I could barely get the words out. "Want to make you proud to be my Master."

"*Fuck.*"

Gage inhaled, and abruptly scissored his fingers. My elbows

gave out and I went forward onto my forearms, moaning, closing my eyes.

"How are you so fucking perfect? It's like someone crafted you especially for me. If I believe in God, I'd... well, it's almost enough to make me believe in God."

I groaned, pushing back on his fingers. "Please Gage, please, I'm ready."

He slapped my ass, right over the stinging section of skin he'd bitten. "You're ready when I say you're ready, puppy. And address me properly."

The spank startled me but it was nothing but pleasure aside from that. I opened my eyes again at the shock of it. "I'm sorry, master."

As if to punish me, he seemed to take an extra long time stretching and prepping me. Adding so much lube it made an obscene sound as he pulled his fingers out and in again.

I knew better than to ask again. Instead I chewed on my lower lip and took it.

Finally he lightly slapped my ass with a lube wet hand. "Ready now. Beg for my dick."

This was a command I'd happily follow. "Please, Master, please please fuck me, I need it. I need you, Master."

He didn't waste time, just gripped my hips and pushed inside. "Are you looking at the locks, Brand?"

Somehow, in all the wash of pleasure, I'd almost forgotten. I refocused my eyes on the golden padlocks and nodded. "Yes, Master." The wave of arousal I got from seeing them was almost more than from him filling me. Almost but not quite.

I imagined a fire alarm going off. There wouldn't be time to find the keys. Gage would have to give me pants and then walk me out of the building chained up. I moaned again.

"Good boy, that's it. Keep on thinking about being my prisoner. My sex toy. Mine, entirely."

He stayed mostly still, letting me adjust to him, rocking his hips only very slightly to get me accustomed.

Now he started to move, gripping my hips tight and using me, just as he'd promised.

The temptation to close my eyes was huge. I'd never paid attention to how much I closed my eyes during sex, aside from when he'd blindfolded me. It turned out to be a lot.

But every time I did, Gage seemed to know. He'd slap my ass, or my hip, yank on my hair.

"Pay attention!" he barked.

I'd obediently look at the locks once more, feeling another surge of arousal. Each time I did, Gage moaned a split second later, feeling my arousal and how it heightened his own.

Neither of us were going to last. I bit my lower lip so hard it bled.

Gage moved even faster, slamming into me. Through the link I could feel his hunger surge.

"Puppy, come for me." He gasped, his hand moving to stroke me, a firm grip making short work of the resolve I had.

"Yes!" I practically shrieked, I was so ready.

He bit my shoulder as I came, drinking a small amount that nonetheless extended out my orgasm in the most incredible way.

Groaning, Gage pulled out a moment later.

I fell forward onto my chest, extending my bound hands out in front of me.

I felt a damp cloth cleaning me. I couldn't stop the contractions, the way my ass wanted to be filled again.

Gage laughed outright.

"It's all right baby, you're gonna be plugged up in just a moment."

True to his word a moment later something cold, hard and slick with lube was pushed into my welcoming hole. I flattened out on the bed, moaning with relief.

"How does that feel so good?"

Gage chuckled. He rubbed my back, easing out some of the tension. "Because you're a wanton slut for me and you can't stand not being stuffed full?"

I was already red from the sex but that comment made my whole body warm. Tingles shot through me, my dick twitching like it still had something to give. He wasn't wrong.

"Well... okay." I mumbled against the bed.

Gage laughed, more fondly this time. I felt the warmth of his affection as his strong hands worked the knots out of my back. It was total bliss.

"That's it, just relax for me, little slut."

"Keep calling me that and I'm gonna want more."

"Mm. Later. Relax, and some food and then we'll go again. Want to make use of this." He tweaked the buttplug.

I jolted.

"You like that?"

I shook my head, and then nodded.

Then I hid my face in the bedclothes as he laughed again.

Once he was satisfied that I was sufficiently relaxed he pulled me up right. "What do you want to eat? Steak? Burger? Whatever you want, I'll get it for you but you have to eat a salad too."

I relaxed against his chest, my head slowly coming out of the sex-fog.

I lifted my wrists, still cuffed and locked together.

"You gonna untie me for dinner?"

Gage nuzzled into my neck. "Nah. You can eat like that just fine."

I squirmed, breathing out heavily so I didn't get aroused again. "Oh."

"Yeah, that's right." Gage gently nipped my earlobe and tugged on it. "Now. What do you want?" He slipped both arms around me while I thought.

I considered it. "Spaghetti, with lots of garlic."

"Ha ha."

"And mushrooms and meatballs." Then I remembered that Gage wanted to spend money on me. Thinking about food had made my stomach rumble. I could probably eat more than just one pasta dish. "Garlic bread, a side of mac and cheese and whatever fancy desserts the pasta place has."

Gage nodded, his jaw grazing against my head, then kissing my damp hair. "Whatever puppy wants, puppy gets."

BRANDON

True to his word, Gage kept me cuffed and locked up
throughout dinner.

He helped me to slip on a pair of designer pajama pants,
which were bamboo cotton but as fine and comfortable as satin.
Then he moved us both into the living room and put the TV on
while we waited for the dinner delivery.

He set up the food on a tray on my lap, but after watching
me struggle through the first bites (two hands cuffed together
isn't the easiest way to spin spaghetti onto a fork), he took pity
on me. I thought he'd undo the cuffs.

Instead, he took the fork and started feeding me.

It probably should have felt humiliating,. In all honesty, it
felt wonderful. He took care of me in the most fundamental way
possible. It was tender, intimate. I relaxed even more into the
role of pet, or plaything, with each mouthful.

It was such a weird thing to be comforted by this. There I
was chained up, plugged, and being fed like a baby, and if Max
had seen this happen he'd definitely have some things to say.
But it wasn't a public thing, this was just Gage being a good
Master and making sure I was looked after. He was soothing me

after an intense session, making sure I rested and got my strength back before the next one. It was wonderful.

Gage was wonderful.

He smiled at me, offering me another forkful of spaghetti. "You're all warm and fuzzy, I can feel it."

"Because of you." I took the mouthful and chewed it, amused to see him squirm for once. "I like this, I like you taking care of me. It makes me feel really, I don't know. Special."

"Yeah well, you bring out my soft side." He looked down and fussed with the garlic bread. "And you are special."

"I like it." I opened my mouth for the next bite, hands resting softly on my thighs. "I like your hard side too. I like it all."

"Good, because you're not getting rid of me any time soon."

After dinner was done Gage insisted I have time to digest everything. He held me while we watched some more TV. After a while, I realized I'd become accustomed to the cuffs, the collar and the padlocks and hadn't been thinking of them in terms of what they really meant. I'd even stopped noticing the plug, which seemed like it should have been impossible to forget.

But the act of realizing it, reminded me what they were there for. I started to feel frisky again.

Gage had his arms around me, one hand resting on my chest. I moved subtly, trying to direct his hand towards my nipple.

"You want something, pet?" He asked, immediately seeing through my plan. I moved again, pressing back against him more firmly, and lifting my chin to kiss his jaw.

"Yeah."

"Insatiable." He moved his hand to squeeze my nipple.

I moaned, arching into his touch.

"You're the one who left me like this with the promise of more."

Gage chuckled, his other hand moving down my stomach to stroke the base of my dick. "You got me there. I like having you ready for me at any time. It's a very nice feeling."

I moaned, rocking into his hand as best I could.

"And you're so ready for me, aren't you? A horny bunny who needs to be fucked?"

Groaning, I nodded. "Yeah."

"Well, no need to wait then." In one impossibly fast movement, Gage slung over his shoulder and stood. I was getting used to this, although I'd have hated it from anyone else, Gage could get away with it.

He carried me to the bed and threw me down on my back. "Want to watch your face this time."

He climbed on top of me and lifted my cuffed hands, securing them to the headboard with a clip there. "Tell me again how much you like being locked up like this."

It wasn't a question, it was a command. He pulled my pants off and then his own as I answered.

"I feel hot. Hot's not strong enough a word. Inflamed. On fire. Like you want me so much you can't risk me getting away, that your desire is so intense you need to possess me. And I love being possessed like this."

Gage hummed. "Good answer. No teasing, let's just go hard and fast."

His hand found the plug and was already tweaking it, starting to loosen it.

I tilted my head back and groaned.

"Yes, Master."

The plug coming out was a welcome feeling but also an excruciating loss. I didn't want to be empty, even for a moment.

Thankfully, Gage meant what he said. Within moments, he pushed into me.

My throat was becoming sore from all the moaning and whining I'd been doing, but it didn't stop me from crying out as he filled me again.

"Eyes on me, bunny." His voice was a low, rough growl, primal and demanding.

I snapped my gaze to his eyes instantly. "What are you, the big bad wolf?"

"Fuck yeah," he said. "And I'm gonna eat you up." No one but Gage could make such a corny line sound hot.

He shoved his hips forward to accentuate this promise and I groaned. Wrapping my legs around his, I pulled him in tighter, moaning as I did so.

"That's it, good boy." Gage rolled his hips, letting me feel every inch of him before he switched gears to relentless pounding.

All I could do was lay back and take it, which was fine because even if I wasn't bound, that would have been all I was capable of anyway.

Mindlessly, I begged him. "Please Master, please please more, please!"

He leaned in and bit my earlobe, growling again. "Insatiable. I love it. You're so good."

His hand wrapped around my dick and pumped it.

I was close to coming after the first stroke.

"PleasecanIcome?" I gasped it out in one breath, sure I couldn't hold it off.

"Yeah." Gage shoved into me. We came in the same moment, almost. Me spurting over his hand and him filling me.

He nuzzled into my neck and I lay there gasping, coming down from the incredible highs of the day slowly.

After a moment, Gage sat up, and pulled out. My hole was sore and used now, and I moaned again, whining at the emptiness even though I knew I needed recovery time.

"Calm down, puppy, you'll be alright." Gage produced small

golden keys and unlocked the cuffs and then the collar. The moment I was free I wrapped my arms around his waist and pressed my face to his chest.

It had been wonderful but now I felt vulnerable and alone.

I wanted to stay his, to be his pet forever. It wasn't a practical desire, and it was also not entirely true. I liked my independence, but the feeling of security, of being taken care of, was intoxicating.

Gage's arms, cold even after a session like that, wrapped around me and held me tight. The strength in his arms was soothing, and after a few minutes of just holding each other, the horrible feeling of loss ebbed away.

"Come on, let's get you cleaned up."

Slowly, gently, and making sure I was all right every step of the way, Gage led me to the bathroom and helped me shower. He got in with me , washing all the sweat and cum off, cleaning out my hole as gently as he could. Through it all I clung him, responding when he asked what I needed and if I was all right.

Then he toweled me dry, helped me into my pajamas and tucked into bed with me.

I was mostly asleep by this point, and I figured I could play it off as something said in a dream. "Love you," I murmured, as loudly as I dared.

Gage pulled me tighter. As I dropped off I thought I heard him say, "Love you, too."

11

BRANDON

A few days later neither of us had said the words to each other again, but I didn't care. I could feel Gage's affection for me. Every time he fed from me, the connection between us got stronger. It meant he felt my affection right back.

I was just finishing up a class, wearing one of my new Superdry shirts, when Gage texted me.

```
Gage: something's come up I need to deal with
   Gage: business thing
   Gage: I'll be out of town a night or two
   Gage: you can still come by my apartment
and eat food, use the TV, whatever. You have
the key, right?
   Brand: Yeah I have the key but
realistically I'll just be at my own apartment
   Gage: ok
   Gage: I'll put food into the freezer if you
change your mind
   Brand: hope it's nothing terrible
   Gage: nah just a stockbroker thing I have
```

```
to go sort out in NYC
    Gage: boring as shit
    Gage: but I have to go like, next
flight out
    Brand: okay
```

The idea that Gage would be out of town was so unexpected that it shocked me. I looked around campus, unsettled. Searching for an answer that wasn't there.

He was such a part of my life now, the idea that I wouldn't see him even if it was just for a couple of nights was outrageous.

I took a deep breath, leaned against a wall outside the building and thumbed my reply.

```
Brand: I'll miss you
    Gage: gross
    Gage: who raised you?
```

I laughed, soothed by his sarcasm. I didn't bother replying because the little icons indicated he was typing again.

```
Gage: I'll miss you too pup
```

I sighed, pocketed my phone and headed back to my apartment.

I found Max sprawled on the sofa in just his boxers, watching a surfing competition. He looked up when I walked in.

"Oh, hey stranger." He raised a glass bottle of kombucha at me.

"Hey." I dropped my bag and sat on the sofa. "You're

looking... fairly casual."

"Well, I got used to living alone." He nudged me with his elbow. "You okay? You look kinda... less than."

"I'm okay. Gage got called away on business all of a sudden. We'd been planning to go see a movie tonight but now I have no plans." I leaned back, propping my head on the edge of the couch. "Which means I'm gonna have to do my coursework. Like a chump."

Max chuckled. "You and me both, brother. Your delightful sister is out of town and has no ETA for her return."

"Sucks, man."

"Well, at least we can study together."

"After the comp coverage is done though. I was thinking of nachos for dinner, unless you have a better idea?"

I considered, but I couldn't remember the last time I'd eaten Max's nachos and that was a travesty. He made the best I'd tasted. "Nachos would be perfection."

Life without Gage in it was the same as it had been before I met him. School, study, eat, sleep. The difference was I wasn't looking around for someone to hook up with. I was still horny all the time but it wasn't like I could go to a party and find a one night stand. I didn't even *want* to do that. I just wanted Gage back.

Max was similarly pathetic, which helped. We commiserated, and laughed at each other, and looked after each other.

Gage's business took him away for more than just two days. On the third day he texted to say there was more to unravel than he expected. We video chatted that night, but he was really distracted and hung up before too long.

I was relieved. We'd never been very good at just sitting and talking face to face. Our big conversations usually happened before or after sex, and over video the distance felt palpable. One hundred times worse.

On the up side, chilling with Max was awesome. I'd missed him, even though I'd been perfectly happy spending time with Gage.

When I told him I had more time before Gage got back, Max suggested a trip to the beach. I agreed instantly.

We went the next day.

Getting some surfing felt incredible. The sea salt on my skin was like an old friend I'd been neglecting. Out there on the ocean with the sun and the sky stretching overhead I felt like my old self, and not just someone pining away for his boyfriend.

It was a good reset and I resolved to do it more often.

Would Gage buy me a car if I asked him?

Telling myself not to be so greedy, I paddled back out for another wave.

On the fourth day of Gage's absence, I headed to class, a spring in my step from surfing the day before. I stopped in at the coffee shop for a bagel.

A shiver went down my spine. Something was off. I'd already ordered and was waiting for them to call my name, so I looked around the place, trying my best not to be too obvious about it.

The weird woman and man were there, and they were both looking right at me. I hurriedly looked away, feeling a thrill of fear. What were their names again? I racked my memory until the answer came: Ford and Shawna.

Gage had said they were vampires.

They were taking a weird interest in me... even stalking me? Apparently?

I glanced at them again. They were in the window booth, her

with a broad-brimmed black hat on, and him in huge sunglasses. They were talking, as if nothing weird was going on.

Did they mean harm?

They gave off a distinctly creepy vibe but I supposed they had only actually been polite to me. Aside from randomly knowing my name.

I reasoned there was nothing they were going to do in broad daylight, in a crowded place.

The staff called out my order. I took the cup and the paper bag, stowing the food in my backpack. I wasn't hungry anymore. I wanted to get out as soon as possible.

As I went to the door, they both stood up.

Ford beat me to the automatic door, gesturing for me to go through first. To anyone watching it would look like a polite, harmless moment. To me it felt like I was turning my back on a predator with designs to devour me.

But I couldn't just *not* walk through the doors. It would be so weird, and I didn't want to stay in the coffee shop either. I had to get to class.

I walked through, nodding my thanks purely out of habit.

They followed me out, of course they did.

I crossed the road, and headed towards campus, lengthening my stride.

I should have known there was nothing I could do to outrun a vampire, even in broad California daylight.

In a heartbeat Shawna was walking alongside me. "So good to see you again, Brandon."

"I wish I could say the same about you. I have class to get to."

She giggled, an eerie sound. "No, you don't."

"Uh, yeah, I do." I glanced at her and wished I hadn't. She wasn't wearing sunglasses and her gaze caught mine. Too late, I remembered the time Gage had used his power of persuasion on me, it had only taken eye contact and a command and I was doing his bidding.

"Brand, you're going to follow me, and you're not going to make any fuss at all. In fact, you're going to act like I'm your oldest friend."

My mind emptied of fear. Emptied of everything.

I had no desires at all, after that. I followed her, I smiled, and we made small talk.

She led me down a side street to a white utility van. Someone I didn't recognize was at the wheel.

I went into the back of the van like a docile puppy and sat still while they handcuffed me to a ring welded into the wall. I even inhaled when Ford pressed a gas mask to my face, because he looked me in the eyes and told me to.

I fell into a dark and dreamless sleep.

Fucking vampire powers.

I have no idea how much time passed.

I woke up slowly, blearily, and looked around. My head was killing me.

I was in a cage in a basement. There was a thin cushion and a blanket, a cot bed and a flushing toilet like in a jail cell. But the cage had bars on all sides, like a large dog cage and it looked solid.

The basement was dim, no doubt a very comfortable light level for vampires. For the moment there was no one else in the room. There were two small windows very high up, street level, probably, on the far wall. The walls and floor were solid concrete.

I rubbed my forehead, my heart was pounding. I didn't like this, not one bit.

I checked myself over next. I had all my clothe. They hadn't stripped me, thank God. That would have been super weird. But the ring Gage had given me for my birthday was gone, along with my phone, wallet, keys and...I felt at my neck. His family crest pendant. They'd taken the two precious pieces of jewelry that linked me to him.

That really pissed me off.

"Hey!" I yelled. "Who are you? Let me go! What is this?"

Nothing but the echoes of my own voice responded. My head felt thick and heavy, a side-effect of the gas Ford had given me, no doubt.

I tried the door, rattled it as hard as I could but it didn't budge. I even tried lifting the cage from within, reasoning that the floor of the cage didn't have bars, but it was far too heavy for me.

I sat down on the cot and closed my eyes, my fear enveloping me. Maybe Gage would feel it and come to my rescue the way he had when those guys beat me up.

But then I remembered with icy clarity that Gage was in New York City. There was no way he was close enough to feel my fear. I hadn't felt anything through the connection since he'd left, so I was all alone.

"I'm fucked." I said to the empty room.

A moment later, the door opened. Shawna walked down the short flight of stairs. She carried a tray. Whatever was on that tray smelled incredible. Someone followed behind her who was hard to make out. They were shrouded in shadow, and I couldn't concentrate on them for long.

"Good morning, Brand, I'm glad to see you've realized the truth of your situation so quickly. If you're a well-behaved little thing, you can eat."

The moment she spoke all my attention dropped from the mysterious figure and I focused on Shawna.

My stomach rumbled audibly, but my jaw set. I looked away from her face, at the floor. I didn't want her to persuade me again.

"I'm not going to be well-behaved."

"I think you are."

She set the tray on a small folding table just outside the door of the cage. The tray held a steaming slice of lasagna, dripping with melted cheese, a large bottle of spring water, a can of coke, and a bowl of salted fries. My stomach rumbled again, demanding the delicious food I could smell.

"I think you'll be hungry enough that you do just what I say so you can eat something."

"What do you even want with me?" I moved closer to the cage door, my feet leading me towards the food despite what my brain said felt safe. "How long was I out for?"

"About eight hours."

Eight hours, and I hadn't even eaten my breakfast bagel. No wonder I was hungry.

"As to what we want from you, well, you have information about a mutual friend, and I want it." She pulled up an armchair and sat down.

If we were going to have a conversation, I would naturally want to look at her, but I shouldn't meet her eyes.

I checked my pockets. They'd taken my phone and wallet, of course they had, but I found a Gucci silk scarf that Gage had insisted on buying me.

I'd pocketed it as a sort of token while he was away. My muzzy mind remembered feeling like he'd be a bit closer, if I reached into my pocket and touched the silk. Well, it had a use anyway.

I pulled out the scarf and blindfolded myself with it.

"Kinky." Shawna laughed.

"At least I'm protected from your fucking magic eyes this way." I leaned against the bars. "I'm not going to tell you anything about Gage, and I'm confident you're not his friend."

"We were friends, once." When Shawna spoke again it was right beside my ear.

I startled back, tripping over the cot in my panic and

crashing to the ground.

Her laughter echoed off the concrete walls. "Well, *that's* certainly a downside to your little plan."

I picked myself up to a sitting position and stayed where I was on the floor. There was no reason to move around, to let her scare me like that. Vampires can move silently and faster than I could detect even with my eyes wide open.

I'd just stay put.

"Fuck you."

Shawna made a prim noise. "I'll go easy on you, boy. First one's free. You can have this meal. But after this, you start talking if you want to eat. You got that?"

There was a dragging noise as she pulled the table closer to the cage.

"I'm not going to tell you anything."

"We'll see. I'll leave you to it, I can't stand watching livestock eat."

Although she could move silently, she didn't bother as she left. Her heels rapped on the floor and up the stairs. When I heard the door close I pulled the scarf tentatively off one eye to check she was really gone. She was.

The basement was empty now, except for myself.

I pulled the scarf down around my neck, ready to replace if she or another vampire came in.

I got up and went to the cage door. I couldn't get a whole plate in between the bars, and they hadn't given me a knife for obvious reasons, but with a little work I could cut bits of lasagna off, spear them on my fork and bring it into the cage to eat.

It tasted even better than it smelled, rich and filling and hot. I ate it quickly, then helped myself to the fries. The bottle of water I could squeeze through, so I finished up the fries and sat on the cot with the plastic bottle, drinking slowly and stopping when it was three-quarters full. I didn't know when I'd be given another bottle after all.

Shawna had called me livestock, which was a horrible thought. Did they keep humans here just to feed on them? Fatten them up like cattle?

How many people had gone missing only to end up here? I shivered, wrapping my arms around myself.

My one comfort was that Gage would notice if I didn't respond to his texts. He'd know there was something wrong. What he would do after that, I had no clue, but I knew he'd come for me. It'd just take time.

Of course, him coming to rescue me was probably a big part of Shawna and Ford's plan... or was it? They'd waited to make their move until he wasn't around after all. Had they been watching, seeing he wasn't around? They might have even meant to do this the day before, but I'd bucked my routine and gone to the beach with Max.

I hoped Max didn't get worried as well.

How would I explain any of this to him? Or to Martina?

Of course, to explain things, I'd have to get out of this alive, and I wasn't sure that would be an easy option.

I wanted to, of course I did, but absolutely nothing was up to me.

Before I opened my eyes I could tell that the kidnapping hadn't been a bad dream.

The room was cold, the bed was hard, and the blanket threadbare. My head hurt still, although the sharpness of the pain had dulled.

I had no idea what time it was. The tiny windows in the walls gave the same amount of light as before. Maybe they just opened onto a hallway?

The lock clicked.

I pulled the blanket over my head.

I didn't know who it was going to be but I didn't want to look them in the eyes.

I felt like a little kid, hiding under the blankets from imaginary monsters, except these monsters weren't imaginary at all.

"Breakfast." Ford's voice. "Lots of protein to build you up. Big boy like you, you probably eat a lot."

I didn't bother responding.

He set the tray of food down. "Now then, no need to sulk. You're our guest for the rest of your life, so you might as well relax and enjoy it. These are waffles from the coffee shop you like so much, with eggs and bacon. And your usual coffee order."

I sniffed the air. It all smelled great. I was sure the coffee would relieve the dregs of my headache.

But Shawna's words from the night before haunted me. *Livestock* first and foremost, but her promise I wouldn't eat unless I gave them information on Gage.

"What's the catch?"

"You can eat, I don't believe in withholding food from prisoners. But nothing is without strings. Eat up, then we'll talk. And you can come out from the blanket. I'll look away if you're that afraid."

I wished I could see his face, although I wasn't at all sure how much I'd be able to read his expression or his intent.

"Is this some good cop, bad cop shit?" The food smelled too good. I emerged, pulling the blanket down tentatively.

Ford sat with his back to me.

Scanning the basement there was a strange shadow in the far corner near the door. I didn't think too much of it.

I made my way to the tray and reached forward, taking a waffle and munching on it. It was lukewarm, but it tasted amazing.

Eating one piece made me hungrier, so I ate some eggs and

downed the coffee. Having food and drink warming me made me bolder, gave me a bit of my old bravado back. The headache fading helped as well.

"Who is usually down here, in this cage?"

Ford didn't move. His voice gave away no emotion. "None of your business."

"Shawna called me livestock. Do you bring humans down here and just feed on them until they're dead?"

Ford didn't respond. I took that as a definite yes.

I closed my eyes and willed Gage to feel my fear. Gage, they'd mentioned him last night.

"What do you care about Gage anyway?"

"You're important to him, that's why we took you. What we want with him won't affect you."

I finished off the food and wiped my mouth on the back of my sleeve.

"I'm not answering shit."

Ford laughed, and turned around then.

I turned my back on him and sat on the bed.

"My friend Shawna is a strange one." He started, his voice amused. "She's a lot more vulgar than I am. Did you know she put her own blood in your dinner last night?"

My blood went icy cold. "What did you say?" If there was vampire blood in the food I'd ingested, then I was on the way to forming a bond with her. I didn't want any vampire blood inside me except Gage's. I wanted a bond with him and him alone... If I accidentally formed a bond with Shawna, would that cancel out the one I had with Gage or would it exist alongside it?

"I think you heard me just fine."

My stomach roiled, hot and unhappy. "What about breakfast?"

"There's nothing in your breakfast. Well, that's assuming you trust me more than you trust Shawna."

I didn't trust either of them as far as I could throw them. I took the two steps to the toilet, knelt and emptied my stomach into it. It was too late for whatever I'd eaten last night but I couldn't risk more infection. I hurled until my stomach was entirely empty.

"That was very dramatic." Ford said dryly. "Well, if you won't eat then we won't have you around as long. It doesn't matter really. Either way you'll lure Gage to us and that's the end goal after all."

I swallowed, looking for the water bottle I'd saved from the night before. The plastic was clear, so I could be sure it was only water. She'd probably hidden the blood in the lasagna, all that red sauce. I groaned and washed my mouth out with a little water, spitting it into the bowl before flushing.

"Fuck you."

Ford chuckled. "Shawna will be down next. She'll try her best to get something out of you. I'd recommend you have a good, hard think about how you would like the last hours of your life to go. We could make it very fun, just as fun as the things you no doubt do with Gage."

"You don't know shit about what I do with Gage."

"Montague told me one or two of the items you purchased recently." Ford tapped the cage bars, making the whole thing hum with a horrible noise. "So I have a few ideas. I could be a very good Master, if you chose to obey me."

"Never." My voice came out as a croak. "You can fuck off and tell Shawna I won't eat anything else she brings me."

Ford laughed darkly.

"Fine. Enjoy your slow, agonizing death."

My bravado lasted until the door slammed and I was alone in the basement again. My stomach contracted and I dry heaved, my heart racing in my temple. Ford had said 'last hours'.

I could only hope that somehow Gage would find me before I was gone. I had no idea *how* he'd do it, but he had to. He had to.

12

GAGE

Brand hadn't texted back.

I'd called but he hadn't answered.

He hadn't messaged to say sorry for missing the call.

He hadn't been online in over forty-eight hours, according to the text just below the picture of him on the chat app we used.

All of these warning signs were too much.

My stockbroker was still trying to play hardball with me. I told him in no uncertain terms that if he didn't get what I wanted done and fast, then I'd find someone who could. He shut up after that. Within hours my bank balance was back where it should have been. The guy thought he could fuck me over because I look young.

I'd have to replace him, but that would wait.

I booked the redeye back to California and paced in the frequent flier lounge, ignoring the cheese platters, the bottles of wine, and the well-to-do giving me the stink eye for being a guy with punk hair and a giant black hoodie who wouldn't sit still.

I needed to get back to Brand. I needed to find out what was happening.

Either he'd decided to break up with me by ghosting, out of the blue, or something was wrong. He was devoted to me. I knew that. I'd felt it every moment we were together. And besides, I'd impressed his sister. There was no reason he'd want to break up.

Which meant he had to be in trouble somehow.

There was an off-side chance he'd lost his phone, but I discounted this immediately. Guys like Brand lived on their phones. If he'd lost his, he'd have grabbed a cheap burner and got in touch.

No.

It was trouble, plain and simple.

They called my flight. I was the first out of the lounge, first seated in business class. I glared at everyone as they came in at a snail's pace. Fussing about their carry-on luggage, whining about leg room.

I should have chartered my own plane, but this had seemed quicker. Bigger planes flew faster after all. Now I regretted it.

If I'd been hungry, well. Things would have gone badly. Impatience plus hungry vampire plus confined spaces weren't a good mix. Thankfully I knew someone in New York who had a supply from the blood bank, so that was fine. I made a healthy donation to the local hospital, as an apology for using some of their supply.

The flight was interminable.

I've never been a patient guy, and even though I knew every moment was getting me closer to Brand, I wanted to scream and start tearing stuff apart.

Finally, *finally* we landed.

"Come on, come on." I could have sprinted through the terminal, but I didn't want to slow myself down with a collision or getting the attention of an airport security guard. So I walked as fast as the fastest human.

I'd left my car in valet parking. I snatched the keys off the valet, threw a fifty at him and got behind the wheel.

Just one problem. Where to go?

The best place to start would be Brand's place, but I'd never actually been there. We always hung out at my place.

Max would know.

That left one immediate problem: How would I find Max?

I hoped I'd be able to sense Brand, but as I drove into the campus area I couldn't sense anything at all.

I caught myself snarling, fangs out. Calm down, you asshole! I couldn't sense shit if I let my agitation run things.

I drove, trying to be as methodical as I could, searching the faces of everyone I saw in case they were Brand or Max or even Martina.

Why hadn't I ever asked Max for his number? Why had I never gone to pick up Brand from home?

Why did I think all I needed was myself?

Why did I think Brand would always be accessible, just because he always had been before?

If I'd been more open, more friendly, I'd have other people I could contact now. I'd have avenues of exploration, rather than just random driving and hoping for the best.

I slapped the steering wheel. "Fucking asshole! Short-sighted dipshit!"

I'd prided myself on being a lone wolf.

On staying away from the vampire community.

Only making brief connections. Now it was well and truly biting me on the ass.

I took a deep breath and tried to think.

There was a coffee shop Brand liked to go to, right? The one where he'd seen...

A wave of dread so intense I thought I'd vomit washed over me.

Those two vampires who'd been creeping on him. Could it

be them? If they'd done something to him I would kill them so hard.

It had to be them.

I pulled the car over and squeezed the steering wheel. I had to be careful not to break it, my vampire strength was unpredictable when I was this aggravated.

Someone knocked on the window of the passenger side, I snarled, baring my teeth at them.

Then I realized it was Max.

I took a moment to steady myself, then wound down the passenger side window. The impression I'd got of him at dinner was a pretty easy-going, optimistic sort but now he looked tense.

"Hey Max."

"Have you seen Brand?" Max demanded.

My heart sank.

"I was hoping you had."

"Fuck." Without being invited, Max pulled the door open and sat down in the passenger seat, pushing the small backpack I'd traveled with into the back. "I haven't seen him in days, I figured you'd come back and he'd gone to see you."

"I just landed" I squeezed the wheel again. "I haven't heard from him in three days."

Max rubbed the bridge of his nose. "This is bad."

"Really bad."

"We should call the police." Max pulled out his phone. "I'm gonna do it right now."

"Wait." I put a hand on his wrist. "Give me a chance to find him first. I have a suspicion about what's happened and if I'm right about it the police won't be able to help."

Max looked at me as if I was spouting nonsense.

Maybe I was.

"Listen. There's something about me, about the connection Brand and I have that you need to know about. I need your help with a starting place, and honestly, any information you have about where he's likely to go. But I'm gonna do some stuff that will seem bugfuck whacky, okay?"

Max crinkled his nose, amused. "Bugfuck whacky? Who talks like that?"

"I'm a vampire." I said bluntly. "I have fangs, too much sunshine burns me, the whole nine yards."

Max blinked at me, then started reaching for the door handle.

I flicked the button that locked the doors. "I'm serious. You want proof?" I popped my fangs and removed my sunglasses, turning my head to show him.

"Fuck." Max's voice broke on his next words "That's why he's been so obsessed. He's like college-boy Bella Swann."

"It's NOT like fucking Twilight, okay?" I huffed and put my fangs away again.

Max actually took the news remarkably well, the same as Brand. Maybe it was the surfer thing, they were just both very practiced at going with the flow.

"So, when I'm close enough, I can sense Brand's emotions. Because of the feeding I've done, it's a whole thing. But I'm not close enough. We need to try and work out where he was... or where he's been taken, so I can be close enough to sense him."

"Who do you think did this?" Max asked. He'd set his phone back on his lap.

"These two asshole vampires. He's seen them around a few times. Weird people, a guy and a girl. They've even spoken to him."

Max pulled a face. "What would they want from him?"

I shrugged, I hadn't thought that far. I just assumed they wanted Brand for the same reasons I did. Because he was beautiful and wonderful and full of blood. Not that blood was a huge motivator for me at this point. I loved Brand for Brand. But when we'd first met at that party, I was definitely about the hot boy with blood aspect.

Maybe it was deeper than that too?

"I'm not big in the vampire scene." I said slowly, not sure how to explain to someone without the context. "Some vampires make covens, or hang out together, some bond for eternity, some have clubs or pubs or... like there's communities. Vampire and magical people communities, right?"

"Sure."

Max cringed back away from me a bit, leaning against the door of the car.

That was a perfectly natural response. I had just shown him I'm a predator and I was definitely agitated, gesturing more than normal.

"I don't do any of that. I live alone. I don't go anywhere to be social. I avoid my own kind. They're assholes, why wouldn't I avoid them, you know?"

"I get that."

"But there's a chance... that the other vampires don't like that. Maybe they think I should be a part of the community. That... I dunno, maybe they think I should pay my dues, or that I'm acting too good for them or. Fuck I don't know. But they could have taken him just to piss me off and lure me in."

Max breathed out heavily. "Okay, yeah. That's really bad."

We sat in silence for a moment, fully taking in the entirety of the badness together.

Max straightened his shoulders.

"I asked around his classes and he hasn't been to them for three days. Whatever happened, it was first thing."

My jaw tightened. "That's good intel. Okay, so what does he do before class?"

"Usually gets something to eat. I know his favorite coffee shop. How about we start there?"

"Perfect." I pulled the car into the road.

Max directed me to the coffee shop. He'd stopped cringing

away from me, since the silent moment. I was quietly impressed behind my wild desperate panic.

I pulled in right outside the coffee shop. The two of us strode in like the stars one of those overly-dramatic cop shows. Me in my huge black hoodie and dark glasses, Max in board shorts and a striped T-shirt, at ten o'clock in the morning.

The stupidest team up you've ever seen.

I was about to stride right up to the front of the queue.

Max put his arm out in front of me, holding me back.

"Let me handle this, yeah?"

I wanted to snarl and shout and fight someone, so what Max said made sense. I nodded once, and we got into the back of the queue. I folded my arms to keep from acting out.

Thankfully for everyone in the place it wasn't a long queue and we were soon at the front.

"Hey there," Max said. "We're looking for our friend, Brand. He comes here most mornings. Do you know him?" He'd brought up a picture on his phone and showed it to the barista.

"Oh yeah. He was here a few days ago but I haven't seen him since."

"How many days? Max asked. "Because neither of us have seen him in three days?"

"Yeah, three days, that'd be right. He didn't come in today or yesterday but he was in the day before. I think he left with two people? But they weren't regulars, I didn't recognize them at all."

I leaned forward over the counter. "Could you describe them?"

"Sure, they were really gothy, all in black and kind of fancy, you know? Maybe some of those steampunk people?"

I groaned.

Max covered the noise by asking for a sandwich and thanking the woman for her help. I paid for it, because he'd been super helpful. Besides, I had money and he was a student.

"I don't suppose you remember which way they left?" Max

asked, as he took his sandwich. "Like, which direction they looked like they were going?"

The woman shrugged. We had to move out of the way for the rest of the people waiting.

"That's something." Max said. "Two steampunk types sound like vampires to me."

I groaned. "Yeah, it does."

"Now we have a starting point."

"If they knew he came here, then they were following his movements." I got back into the car, trying to push away my anger and fear and think clearly. "That means they'd know not to keep him somewhere too close because I'd sense him."

"Unless they want you to find him?" Max said. "Then they'd just sit with him somewhere obvious and wait for you."

"Obvious." I repeated. I thought harder. Thought about what little I knew of the local vampires. There was a club downtown, wasn't there? I usually avoided that whole block because there were always vampires...

"I have an idea. Let's try it."

13

GAGE

The club wasn't open this time of day. In fact it had just closed. Would there be cleaners inside?

If only I'd come in at least once or twice, got to know some of the people who ran it. Then I'd be in a better position to investigate the place.

We were parked across the street, watching the door. It had old-fashioned wooden doors that opened outwards from the middle, like a fucking medieval castle. Over the top to say the least.

There wasn't a sign or any advertising, aside from a little over the door wooden thing that said "V."

"Club V," I muttered. "So pretentious."

Max snorted. "You think he's in there?"

"I'll see if I can tune in. Stay quiet." I closed my eyes, took a breath I didn't need, and tried to empty out the anger and fear again. It rushed back the second I got rid of it. I licked my teeth. I could do this. It was for Brand. If I could find him then this would be over.

There.

A faint, tiny niggle.

Brand was tired, and very, very afraid.

"He's here." I opened my eyes. "It's faint. I don't know if that means there's magic over the place, or he's not as close as we'd like, or—" I cut myself off.

"Or what?" Max demanded.

"Or he's ... close to death." I swallowed. "There's no telling which it is, but the connection is weaker than I'd like. You stay here."

"The hell I will." Max undid his safety belt.

"Max, it's going to be very dangerous for humans. Vampires won't hesitate to hurt you, maybe even kill you. I can't keep an eye on you and get Brand out safely."

Max huffed. "I can't just sit in the car and wait! I'll go nuts!"

"I hate to do this but..." I pulled my sunglasses down and looked him in the eyes. "Stay here, don't panic. I'll bring him back. You just relax, got it?"

His eyes went glazed as the vampiric enchantment took hold of him. "Yeah."

I went to get out of the car and then paused. "If someone comes out of that door who isn't Brand, or me, start the car up and drive around the block okay?"

"Yeah."

I left the keys in the ignition, switched the radio on and hopped out. Max slid into the driver's seat, which wasn't technically one of the commands I'd given him but was good preparation if needed.

I leaned back in before closing the door. "If Brand comes out without me, take him to the nearest hospital, got that?"

"Yeah, duh," Max said.

I was pleased he wasn't *totally* undone by the enchantment. That happened with some people. He still had his faculties, he just had my goals infused into his immediate to do list now.

I tugged my hood further over my face and crossed the road. The street was quiet this time of day, but one or two people walked past. I waited for them to be far enough away not to notice if I did something weird.

I got the door and tried it.

Locked.

I tried it again with my vampire strength.

The handle snapped off. Open.

"Right." I tipped my head back as I popped my fangs and summoned all the rage and blood in me to the surface. My powers would work better if I let them bubble close to the top. "Into the belly of the beast."

14

BRANDON

On the second day they started to feed from me.

It was a different from when Gage did it.

I fought, of course, but there's only so much a human could do against two — Or was it three? — Determined vampires who had you locked in a cage.

I was a big guy, but they had superpowers and a steep advantage.

I could tell when Ford and Shawna bit me but sometimes it seemed there was a third person... Vampire, but maybe there wasn't because I never saw a third face.

My mind was muzzy from lack of food.

I lost track of time.

I slept a lot. I didn't know how long had passed.

They stopped asking about Gage.They had cared intensely about him for a day and then gave up and switched to using me as a personal buffet.

So, I slept.

Sometimes, when Shawna came down she'd kick the cage until I woke up. Then she'd come into the cage, grab me and bite. Usually on the neck, which hurt like fuck. Sometimes on the bicep, sometimes leg.

It was always agony.

I screamed. I cried. After the first few times I stopped struggling. It hurt more if I tried to get away.

Ford just grabbed my arm through the bars and bit. I don't know how many times I woke up to the pain of his fangs in my flesh. I started to fear sleeping, but I had no energy to stave it off.

They left less food, less often, because I wouldn't take anything which wasn't in a sealed package, or a clear bottle of water. They didn't care about my nutrition or keeping my strength up. They just took.

Gage always licked where he'd bitten, to make the wounds heal.

These two never did.

They bit, they drank, then they discarded me like a takeaway coffee cup. It was every nightmare humanity ever had about vampires. The word *'livestock'* kept reverberating around in my head. Sometimes it was the only thing I could think of.

The outside world seemed so distant. It couldn't be *too* long since they'd taken me. Surely not as much as a week, but the intensity of my situation was such that it had become my whole world.

I didn't see anyone but Ford and Shawna.

Didn't know anything but sleep, be bitten, sleep. Maybe eat if they'd taken pity on me and given me a sealed granola bar, maybe drink water... but mostly sleep and pain.

My dreams were fitful. Mostly of dying, drained to death by these two vampires. I dreamed the bond between Gage and I was gone, replaced by a link to my captors.

When I was awake, I was so numb I couldn't tell if I'd developed a bond with Ford or Shawna. I couldn't feel Gage, I knew that for sure.

I woke up with a start from the cruelest dream of all — the dream that Gage swept me into his arms and took me back home. It felt so real, so wonderfully soft and warm. He fed me, bathed me, called me his precious puppy.

I woke with tears soaking my cheeks. Fuck. How could I waste water on crying? I had nothing to spare.

Shawna walked down the stairs, a large bottle of water dangling from her hand. She smirked as she saw me swiping at my face.

"Aw, are you sad, sweetie? I've got you a nice drink of water. Ford was complaining that your blood was getting brackish."

I rolled my eyes, feeling a smidgeon of sass rising. "God forbid my life's blood isn't completely palatable to you when you fucking force it out of me."

"Play nice now." Shawna paused at the cage door. "Or I won't give you the water, and Ford can suffer. Personally, I like it when the blood starts flowing sluggish. It tastes like death is near. Delicious."

I shuddered, but I couldn't tear my eyes from the bottle of water. It had to be several pints worth. I sat down on the bed and held out my hand.

The action reminded me I hadn't washed in days. My armpits were rank, and my T-shirt practically stuck to me.

The T-shirt Brand had bought me. My precious Master. He was so generous and kind... and now I was probably going to die wearing this ruined shirt. Without his ring or his family crest.

"Good boy." She opened the cage door, smirking like a cat who got the cream.

I shuddered again. "Don't say that."

"Why not?" She locked the cage door behind her and sat beside me, taking hold of my arm in her iron grip. "No one else is ever going to call you a good boy but me. Why not embrace it?"

"Fuck you." The words didn't hold much power. She was already drinking more of what precious blood I had left and my head was swimming. I leaned back on the cage bars and closed my eyes.

Part of me wished this was all over one way or another. I'd learned how to not struggle when her teeth pierced me, but I still felt every bit of flesh as it tore.

15

GAGE

I stepped through the doors, finding myself in a large, opulent lobby. All red velvet and gold-plated candelabras with a huge mahogany desk like an old-school hotel reception.

The Brand connection was a stronger now, although he was still far away, or weakened.

"Excuse me, you can't just barge in, we're not open yet." A tall woman, no, a vampire, with a regal look about her and a long black ponytail glared at me. The broom she was holding slightly undercut her impressive scowl.

"Yeah, well someone very important to me is being held here." I walked towards the '*Staff only*' door.

She was in front of me in an instant, fangs bared. "No entry."

I stopped, pulled my sunglasses off and pocketed them. "You're more bothered by me coming in before opening time, than the fact that someone's been fucking kidnapped and held here?"

She blinked. "Wait, what?"

"Yeah." I folded my arms. "So are you going to let me through to find him, or what?"

"No one here has been kidnapped. In fact there's no one

here. Just me, the bartender and a couple of janitors." Her brow furrowed in a pretty way, If I was into girls she'd be just my type.

"Bad news, lady."

"Athena." She side-stepped to block my way again. "Tell me what's going on."

"Athena, hi. My boyfriend, a human. I can sense him. Blood bond. He's close. I can't sense him anywhere else. Now, get out of my way because I'm going through there no matter what."

"Humans aren't allowed to come here unescorted," she said. "If he's here he must have come in with someone... But he's not here, all the rooms are checked at dawn when we close."

"Let. Me. Through."

She set the broom against the wall and nodded, pushing the door open. "Follow the bond. Let's see what we find."

Through the door was a hallway, no carpet or lush lighting like in the entranceway to the club.

I made my way through the back rooms, sniffing Brand out like a bloodhound.

Literal bloodhound, I snorted to myself. I felt elated as the sense of him grew stronger, but no matter how many rooms I looked in, once it got to a certain point it got no stronger. I sniffed in circles and lost patience.

"Is there another level?" I turned back to Athena.

She'd been texting as she followed me around. Possibly summoning the vampire police to arrest me for being pushy and spouting off about my human boyfriend. Whatever, there were no laws against it.

"Yes, there's a floor downstairs where the playrooms and dungeons are, then a mezzanine where some of my workers hang out on the job."

"Dungeons." I was so incredulous the question just came out like a statement of disbelief.

"BDSM dungeons, yes. They've all been cleared, cleaned and

98

reset though, I did that myself this morning because Gemini went home early."

I rubbed my forehead. "Take me down there. I've got a read on him but it's not getting stronger. I assume the mezzanine isn't big enough to hide a whole person?"

"That's right."

She took me back out into the club proper, through the bar area, past the dance floor and the booths that lined the walls and down a wide staircase to the lower level. The sense of Brand got stronger by a fraction along with a strange niggle. A vague feeling of wrongness I couldn't define. Maybe the club had one of those sound-based deterrents and I was reacting to that. It didn't matter. Only Brand mattered.

"Closer," I said.

We walked through the various playrooms. Athena hadn't been lying. The rooms were open and clean enough that it was clear no one was secretly being kept there. But again, the link to Brand increased a touch and then not again.

"There has to be a level below this."

Athena frowned, her red lips screwing to the side. "The cellar, but it's been locked and boarded up for years. No one goes there."

"Someone has." I swallowed. Imagining Brand being kept in a boarded-up cellar tore at my heart. I'd get him out. He'd be in the sunlight soon.

"Okay. If you're lying about all of this I'm going to kick your ass though. You haven't even told me your name."

"It's Gage." I raised my eyebrows. "Can we hurry? "

"Wouldn't kill you to use some manners, Gage." She rolled her eyes and led the way to a side door, painted as black as the corridor wars. Three boards nailed across it were soon torn down. The door itself was locked, and she took a moment to find the correct key.

I was impatient but Athena, although she was doubtful, was

being an ally right now. Lashing out at her made no sense, it'd slow me down even more.

I sucked in rage and irritation as she sorted through her ring of keys and closed my eyes, tuning into the faint thread of Brand.

"Thanks. Please. Sorry."

He was closer. Close, but not close enough.

Finally, Athena opened the door to the basement and it swung open with a creak.

The door opened onto a dingy corridor and another, closer door.

Something rustled.

I ran through the second door, finding myself on a flight of concrete stairs. I paused, giving myself a moment to take in what I was seeing.

The basement was completely empty. Four dilapidated concrete walls. A floor bare of anything except a couple of vintage-looking wooden crates, and ancient bits of paper rubbish.

But I could sense Brand nearby, stronger than I had in days. I could practically smell him.

Beside me, Athena looked as confused as I felt. Her ponytail swished as she looked back and forth.

The noise. I heard it when the door first opened. Now it appeared the entire space was empty. Just dust and not even any rats.

"Something's off. I don't like this." I strode down the stairs. Thinking of nothing but the fact that Brand was close.

I felt his pain, throbbing in my skull. His fear like an ache in my own muscles.

Nothing would keep me from him.

"The room doesn't make sense." Athena was right behind me. "It should be bigger than this, deeper. The back wall should be at least ten feet back, towards the street, and have windows. You can see them from the outside."

I hissed a guttural, animal sound. The unpleasant niggle at the back of my neck was the presence of magic. I hadn't felt it often enough to recognize it the second it kicked in, but I knew it now.

Someone was using magic to keep me from Brand.

I would kill them.

But I couldn't get through. Whatever the magic was, it was powerful enough that the illusory back wall wouldn't let me through. The false back wall was as solid as if it was concrete.

"How do I break it?" I faced Athena, seething. "He's here. I can feel it, and he's in pain. He needs me."

Athena's eyes flicked up at me and then back to the phone in her hand. She was scrolling, tapping, then scrolling again. "One second. I'm on it."

It was near-impossible to hold myself back from lashing out at her. I managed it, but only just. Athena was an ally. Tearing her arm off wouldn't help Brand. I paced back and forth, tracking a tight loop in the dust.

She tapped the phone decisively. "There. Should take effect soon."

Somewhere above us, I felt another wave of magic. It pulled at my stomach like I was going to throw up, something I hadn't done since I was a human. A sensation I didn't miss.

My confusion and discomfort cut through the anger for a split second. "You have an app for magic?"

"It's my security system. It should start working—"

Before she could finish her sentence the false wall illusion fell away like a curtain coming down on a stage.

I could see him. Smell him. Hear him.

Brand.

My Brand.

He was in a fucking cage.

His head lolled to one side, whimpering as that hellfiend vampire woman drank from his neck.

The tall man was there as well but I barely noticed him. In the back of my consciousness I heard Athena say something but it didn't matter. My body moved with lightning speed barrelling towards the cage. A roar erupted from me. My fangs were out, they felt larger and more powerful than they'd ever been before.

"Let go of him! I'll kill you!"

The cage door was closed and locked but fueled by my rage and the animal need to rescue my mate, my Brand, my vampiric strength seemed to be at Incredible Hulk levels.

I tore the cage door off its hinges. Metal screeched as I ripped it free and tossed it against the concrete floor.

An icy blast of wind hit me from behind.

I fell to one knee, just outside the cage door. I turned to look for the source.

A tall vampire man with weird pale blue lights around his hands snarled at me. He was dressed like a Victorian gentleman.

"You think you're too good for us, do you?" His voice twisted in a scream. "Think you can hunt how and where you like? That you can ignore centuries of—"

I didn't care what this guy had had to say. I launched myself at him, fangs bared and my hands curled into claws. he crumpled to the ground. I was on him within a second intent on ripping his throat out.

Behind him stood Athena with a stun gun in her hand.

Had she had that on her this entire time? Badass.

I wasted no time. The icy magic was gone from his hands but there was no telling for how long. I tore his throat clean out of his body. I spat it to one side, further enraged by the familiar taste of Brand's blood mixed in with the vampire's.

I would have gone further, torn his head off, or pried open his ribcage and eaten his heart, but a familiar whimper that caught my attention.

Brand.

He needed me.

I moved faster than I ever had before, surging into the cage with a growl, ready to kill the vampire woman the way I'd killed her mate.

I stopped short.

She had moved with similar speed to me and held Brand up with a hand on the back of his neck.

"Stop where you are, or I kill him."

Brand looked terrible. His skin was gray and the bags under his eyes took up most of his cheeks. His cheeks were sunken, sallow. The way his shoulders slumped and his head lolled on his neck told me he wouldn't have been standing if she wasn't holding him up.

My perfect, sun-golden surfer boy looked like a puppet with its strings cut. My heart ached. His blood seeped from the wounds on his arm and neck. One more bite would finish him off.

My baby boy was holding on by the barest thread.

I hesitated. I wanted to take him in my arms but I didn't want her to strike. I had to protect him, but how?

"What the fuck are you doing in my basement, Shawna? You had your final warning, already."

"What do you want." I grated the words out, holding myself still with monstrous effort. I'd never held myself back like this before. I couldn't tear my eyes off Brand.

He didn't seem awake enough to have noticed me. His bright eyes were dull and unfocused. I wondered if he was even aware of what was going on.

"Gage." Athena's was trying to warn me of something. I ignored her.

Shawna rolled her eyes. "You idiot. I just want to take what's yours."

"But why? I don't fucking know you."

"I'm your sister, Ford was your brother. You've killed your own kin."

I shook my head, utterly confused. "I don't have brothers and sisters."

"Same sire?" Athena ventured. She was still on her phone, tapping and scrolling. What tricks did she have stored in there that might come into play shortly?

"Yes, the same sire." Shawna spat on the ground. "And Gage has rebuffed every possible chance to get to know us, to be a family. To share the wealth he's accrued. He has been cruel, selfish and heartless. So we took the thing he really loved."

Athena tutted. "You're idiots."

"Just give me Brand back," I said through gritted teeth, "and I'll give you money, if that's what you want. I'll give you anything."

"Too late. You already killed Ford."

"Come on." I huffed. "If you kill him, I kill you. There's no way out of that. You're backed into the cage. Either you take my offer or you die."

Shawna pulled Brand closer to her, causing him to moan softly.

"I want more than money." She said slowly, as if she was only just forming the thoughts as she spoke them. "I want to be in your life, live as your sister. Together we can rule the night."

"For crying out loud," Athena muttered behind me.

"Of course, whatever you want. Just give him back." I gritted my teeth around the lie.

"You mean it?" she eyed me, a feral dog suspicious but hoping to trust.

I moved closer, held out my hand as if to shake on it. "For the rest of your life I'll treat you as a sister."

She shuffled a little, moving Brand to one side to reach out to me.

She took my hand.

In an instant, I was on her. One arm wrapping around Brand to stop him falling, the other pulling her close to break her spine. Then I bit deep into her neck, sucking down the precious traces of Brand I could taste.

Shawna didn't even fight, really. She just sighed happily and died as I drained her.

I dropped her on the floor.

"Cold. I like it." Athena moved to take Brand.

I rounded on her, snarling.

"He's mine!"

She raised her hands. "Yeah Beast Boy, I got that much. Not trying to take him from you, just help you out a bit. How about you calm the fuck down and we get him to a hospital?"

Brand's scent went some way to soothing me, and the fact I had my arms around him cemented the truth in her words. I didn't need to fight Athena. In fact she'd suggested something essential.

"Right, yes." I blinked as the monstrous rage inside me melted into pure fear. Brand wasn't out of the woods. "I could give him some of my blood...?"

"Unless you want to turn him, I don't think that's a good idea." Athena led the way out of the basement. "The amount he needs at this stage is too great."

I lifted Brand into my arms and winced at how light he felt. "You're right. Hospital and transfusion. I have someone waiting with a car outside."

Athena led me out the short way.

I rushed Brand into the car, settling him on my lap in the back seat. Max had already started the car and was pulling out. "Emergency room, yeah?"

"Yeah."

Max drove and I held Brand, unable to look away from his face. Had I done enough? Had I come too late?

I didn't want to consider what would happen if I'd come too late. Despair tugged at me, ready to consume me, but I wouldn't let it in.

What mattered was Brand.

I wanted to shake him, to bring him back to life with the sheer force of my need, but that wouldn't have done anything but hurt him. I gripped him as tightly as I dared and willed him to hang on.

"Please stay with me, Brand," I said. I didn't care if Max heard. "I know it's hard, but please, I need you so much. I love you. I need you. Stay with me."

16

BRANDON

I'd had another of those horrible dreams. A dream where Gage rescued me.

I could barely open my eyes, I was so weak. Why bother? I didn't need to know that the walls around me were steel bars. That I was about to be fed on by someone who didn't care how much pain they gave me.

Gradually, I became aware that the sounds around me weren't what I expected.

Something gently beeped. I could hear muffled voices nearby. Voices I didn't recognize. Voices that weren't Shawna and Ford.

I forced my weary eyelids up and immediately shut them again. The room was so bright!

Opening them a slit, I looked around. Sterile white walls, a blanket, tubes coming out my arm and from under my shirt... I was still wearing the filthy shirt I'd been wearing for days but underneath that were electrodes and monitoring devices.

I was in hospital.

Or I was dead and heaven began with a very realistic hospital scenario. What was more likely?

My bed was curtained off. Ass I opened my eyes more fully, I saw the shadows of people moving behind it.

I tried to say hello, to alert someone that I was awake. All that came out was a dry cough.

In an instant the curtain was pulled open. Gage was there, his hand on mine, his eyes shining.

"Brand. You woke up."

"I..." My throat hurt like sandpaper.

"Don't try to talk or sit up." A new voice, a nurse, who barely came up to Gage's shoulder, bustled forward on the other side of the bed. "You've been through a lot. How's your pain?"

My pain?

I took a mental stock. Every part of me hurt. It felt like my entire skin was wounded, and my bones felt bruised.

"Achey? Bad."

Gage gently squeezed my hand.

The nurse wrote something on a clipboard. "I can give you more pain relief. It's best if you sleep as much as you can while the IVs do their work."

I craned my head, looking at the plastic bags that slowly dripped into my arm.

Gage leaned down and pressed the softest of kisses on my forehead. I could have cried but I was too tired. No tears would come anyway.

"What's... what's IVs?" I slurred out.

"You're on a blend to rehydrate you. Lots of vitamins and some potassium and sodium supplements. I'm about to put in a dose of morphine so you can sleep again."

Gage leaned in and kissed my cheek. "I love you, Brand."

I heard that.

I knew he'd saved me. It hadn't been a dream, not that last time. My hero. "Love you."

I slipped back into unconsciousness, smiling for the first time in an eternity.

The next time I woke up I felt noticeably better. I had no idea how much time had passed, but the pain had reduced and my head felt clearer.

I opened my eyes to find I'd been moved to a private room. A clean hospital gown had replaced my dirty shirt. A vase of fresh flowers sat on the windowsill and my sister, Martina, snored gently on the one armchair.

"Hey Marty." My voice was still scratchy as all hell, but I wanted her to know that I was awake.

She opened her eyes and smiled. "Hey, yourself. How are you feeling?"

"Bit better." I yawned and stretched my legs out. "How long have you been here?"

Martina checked her watch. "Few hours. I sent Gage home because he'd been hovering endlessly. I don't think he even slept."

I snorted a little. "How long has it been?"

"You were brought in three days ago." Martina came closer, brushing my hair back off my forehead. "You really gave us a scare, baby brother. Gage said you were taken by a cult?"

"Sounds about right." I closed my eyes, enjoying the gentle affection. "It wasn't fun."

"Try not to think too much about it. Your only job is to rest and heal. Max has gone to your professors to let them know why you're missing classes and stuff."

I couldn't imagine thinking about school right now. "Tell him thanks?"

"Oh and Gage left this for you." I opened my eyes. She pointed at a new phone, sitting on a charging pad on the bedside table. "He said to get in touch as soon as you're up for it. Although, I'm sure he won't stay away for long. That boy has it bad for you."

"Yeah." I couldn't remember any details, but I knew he'd come to find me. He was my hero, and I loved him. "I have it bad for him too."

"Get some more sleep, Brand. Either me, Max or Gage will be here when you wake up again. If you get better soon I'll get you a Matchbox car."

Matchbox cars. My mother always got me cars when I was sick. My mouth tugged into a smile.

My eyelids were already drooping from the effort of speaking full sentences, so I didn't respond, just closed my eyes and drifted off.

When I woke up, Gage was back.

For a moment I just watched him. Even in the harsh hospital lighting he looked handsome. The curtains on my window were drawn so I suspected it was nighttime. He wore a black and red checked shirt and artfully ripped black jeans. His hair looked like he hadn't washed it and it hung down over his forehead.

I went to sit up.

The moment I rustled the sheets he was up and beside me.

"Don't move too much, pup, you're still hurt."

"I feel a lot better," I said. "I guess the IVs did their job."

"Yeah. You had a lot of transfusions before that too, those would have helped." He took my hand, the one which didn't have the line in it, and rubbed it gently with his thumb. "What do you need?"

"Wanna sit up."

He produced a remote with three buttons on it. "Your bed will sit up for you."

"How about that?"

After some trial and error, I had the bed arranged in a comfortable way, and I felt almost human again.

Gage didn't say anything. He sat down next to my legs, watching me and holding my hand.

The bond between us was weakened. I couldn't feel what he was feeling, and that, more than the fact I'd almost died, was disconcerting.

"I'm sorry," Gage said finally. "I should have been around."

I shook my head once, regretting it when the room spun briefly. "No, I'm sorry. I should have... I don't know. Taken them more seriously when I noticed them around."

"Shut up." His tone wasn't very serious. "You don't apologize for being kidnapped. That's ridiculous."

"Okay, then you don't apologize for going away to handle work things."

He groaned and looked away, finally nodding. "That seems sort of fair."

"More than sort of."

Gage leaned down, kissing the back of my hand. "I thought I was going to lose you. I never want to feel that way again."

"No." I couldn't meet his eyes, so I dropped my gaze to his hand on mine. "I was sure they'd kill me. They started off asking about you and then they just switched to feeding... all the time." An involuntary shudder went through me. I bit my lip. "I'd given up."

"Max and I teamed up to find you," Gage said.

I looked up. I hadn't expected that. I'd assumed Gage would have called Max and Martina after the rescue, once I was safe in hospital.

"You did? How did that go?"

"I told him what I am. Had to use compulsion to keep him in the car while I went to find you."

I snorted. "Has he told Marty?"

"No idea," he said. "But she hasn't treated me any different. He took it in stride, though."

I leaned back against the pillows. Nothing ruffled Max, even

111

the existence of literal vampires. It made sense. "When can I eat?"

"As soon as you want to." Gage gestured to the call button. "The doctors want you to eat and drink if you feel up to it. Just press the button and someone will come."

I pressed the button, my stomach had begun to tell me just how long it had been since I'd had a good meal.

"Gage, can you... not in detail, just give me the Cliffs notes. What actually happened? Where did they take me? How did you find me?"

Gage's expression had been soft and concerned, now it hardened. "They had you in the basement of a vampire BDSM club."

My eyebrows shot up. "What?"

"Yeah. The owner had no idea. She'd already banned the two of them for life for shitty behavior but they found an alternate way in through this disused speakeasy tunnel. And they used a whole lot of powerful magic to cloak themselves."

"I thought..." My head throbbed. Was a third person involved? Someone had driven the van, hadn't they? "There was a third vampire. I don't know how much they were there."

"A third?" Gage scowled.

"Someone drove the van when they took me. And sometimes there was a strange shadow. I never saw it clearly and it seemed to come and go at random."

"Fuck...Probably my sire." Gage plunged his face into both hands and groaned from the depths of his soul.

I shivered, unsure what else to say.

Gage shook himself and sat back up. "Anyway, Athena knows about it now and she's thinking of doing it up, making it a proper part of the club."

"Athena?" I pulled the blanket further up my chest, feeling a chill.

"The owner. She helped me out. We're...." he hesitated. I

waited, totally unsure what he was about to say. "We're friends now."

I was about to respond when a nurse bustled in.

"Ah good, you're awake. She was an older woman, maybe my mother's age, with red hair peppered with white strands, she peered into my eyes. "How are you feeling?"

"Hungry."

"Good." She beamed at me. "We'll get some food up straight away. Nothing too exciting to start with, just soft foods and soups until your stomach gets accustomed again, but we'll make sure it's tasty."

"Thanks, doc."

She asked me a few more questions, checking my pain levels, flashing a light, asking if I knew the president's name and so on. Soon, food was brought in and I started to eat.

It wasn't long before I'd had enough to eat and set the tray aside.

Then I recalled the other things that had been taken from me. I looked at my hand, pale, hospital bracelet, nothing else. A pang went through me.

"They took my ring, and your crest." This, of all the things we'd talked about made the tears well up. "I guess... they weren't found?"

"No." Gage's voice was soft. "It's all right, pup. I can get you new ones, no problem at all."

"But they were from you and they took them." Tears flowed out my eyes, soaking my cheeks and my hospital gown.

"You'll have new ones."

Gage climbed into the bed beside me.

He wrapped his arms tightly around me. I put the mattress back into a flat position.

After a while the tears dried, soothed by his steadfast presence.

I could feel the IV in my arm. Gage's shoulder was boney under my head.

The bed wasn't big enough for the both of us and I was in danger of rolling off.

It was the most comfortable I thought I'd ever been. I fell asleep, awkwardly pressed into his arms.

17

BRANDON

They kept me in hospital for a few more days. I got better quickly. The doctors put it down to my youth and my relative physical fitness before the incident.

Martina brought me six Matchbox cars. I honestly think they helped me get better quicker, too. Driving them up and down the blankets when I got bored of TV made Gage laugh, and his laugh made me feel better every time.

Gage took me home with him, fighting off Martina and Max with his insistence that he could easily work from home and therefore be available for whatever I needed.

I didn't argue. I wanted to sleep in his giant bed, and touch him all over, and more than anything else shower in his bathroom. The hospital shower just didn't cut it. I was too spoiled now.

One morning, I woke up to Gage was beside me, sound asleep.

Did vampires sleep? I didn't think I'd never seen him sleep before. Maybe it was a vampiric thing, a slumber or temporary death thing?

At any rate, he wasn't conscious.

I'd nearly died. My bones ached still, and I felt weak, not like myself.

I looked at Gage. This entire ordeal was because of him. It wasn't his fault, I didn't blame him, but it had absolutely happened because of our relationship.

I loved Gage. I loved being with him. I'd never felt as accepted or understood as I did with him.

But was it worth it?

Was I always going to be in danger from now on? How many other vampires had Gage pissed off?

There was the shadowy memory of a third vampire, back in the basement. Gage and Athena had only killed two, from their report.

Who was the third, and where were they now?

Was it really Gage's sire, out to hurt him through me?

How long would it be before they came out of the shadows again and tried something on me?

I shuddered, pulling the blanket further up my shoulder as if it was the cold and not the dreadful thought that had given me that reaction.

That was the risk I had to consider.

Dating a Hallowe'en monster like a vampire, things weren't ever going to be easy.

But was it too dangerous to endure, or was it worth it? Was Gage worth it?

I considered cutting ties with him. Telling him to leave me alone.

The emotional link between us was weak, from the other vampires feeding off me. It would be the perfect time to bail.

I could do it.

But then what would I do?

I'd miss him. I knew it deep in my bones. I'd miss him like

my chest had been split open and my heart removed, that kind of missing.

I didn't want to be without him. His sly humor, his sharp wit, the way he looked after me, the way he wanted me to be happy. I wanted to see where this went.

Would it be worth the risk?

There was no way of knowing.

Gingerly, I stroked a fingertip across his cheekbone. He twitched, as if annoyed. I pulled my hand back. Not fake dead then.

Realistically, no relationship was a guaranteed success.

No one could say for sure that what they had was worth everything, that it would never change for the worse. Uncertainty was part of what made love so appealing.

It was a leap of faith every time.

So, then the question was, would I do that leap of faith for Gage?

The answer came immediately.

Yes.

Yes, I would. I'd do it again and again because I loved him, and I wanted to be with him.

It was a relief to have that answer.

I realized how tense I'd been as I considered it all. I took a deep breath and let it out slowly, relaxing as my muscles eased

Gage blinked awake. His forehead creased as if the world offended him by allowing him to wake up.

"You okay?"

"Yeah." I cupped his cheek and relaxed further. "I'm awesome."

The days stretched out and I slowly healed.

Gage was a fussy nurse, insisting that I stay on bed rest even though the doctors hadn't encouraged that. My energy levels weren't quite back up to normal, so sprawling on the couch watching TV was perfectly fine.

I got deep into the *Great British Bake Off*. I dozed on the couch while Gage worked on his laptop and stroked my hair.

At night he'd come to bed with me and stay until I fell asleep, holding me.

The first time Gage took me out of the house it was just to go to the store and pick up some food. He had been ordering in, which was far safer, but I wanted to see some sunlight. This seemed like a good, innocuous first trip.

Gage pulled on a gigantic black hoodie and dark glasses and I pulled on pants that weren't sweatpants for the first time in weeks.

It was a short walk. I was glad to stretch my legs. I breathed in the fresh air and exhaled it with a whoosh. "This is exactly what I needed."

Gage took my hand and squeezed it.

"Good." He was vigilant, looking all around us as cars drove past.

It occurred to me then that there was something to be looking out for, and my shoulders hunched. Was someone watching us right now? Someone who wanted to do something terrible to me? Or worse, to Gage?

I shivered and moved closer to Gage so our shoulders touched.

"It's okay," Gage said.

"You think?" I scanned the area but couldn't see anything out of the ordinary. I realized I was looking for Shawna, but of course, she was gone. I didn't have to worry about her ever again, just... whoever that third vampire had been. Gage's sire? I had no idea what he looked like beyond shadows. He must have vampire magic to be able to hide himself like that.

"Yeah." Gage tugged my hand and led me into the convenience store. "You can buy whatever you want but remember you have to carry it back."

"Not a problem."

Gage had already stocked the fridge with my favorite flavors of sports drinks, but I grabbed some soda and lots of snacks, potato chips, bags of candy, granola bars, and chocolate. Why the hell not? I grabbed some peanut butter crackers and a big jar of Nutella to finish off.

Gage rolled his eyes. "For the love of... there's a reason I make you eat vegetables and this is it right here."

I grabbed an apple pie from the shelf. "There, now I'm getting fruit."

"Fruit soaked in sugar and wrapped in butter pastry doesn't count, Brand."

"Does too."

Gage paid for it all, and to my surprise produced a couple of fold-up reusable shopping totes from his pocket to load it all into.

He caught my look of incredulity and shrugged. "What? Saving the planet is punk rock."

I didn't have a response to that.

On the walk home I felt more assured, swinging a bag of groceries Gage had bought me (he had the other two, despite his earlier threat to make me carry it all.)

I jumped out of my skin when a car horn sounded close by. Gage, apparently just as on edge as I was, despite looking outwardly cool, pressed me against the wall of the nearest shop, shielding me with his body.

The car drove on. Absolutely nothing happened, but my heart was thundering.

"You know, we've never actually been on a date."

Gage looked up at me. He'd been reading a novel while I watched more of the *Great British Bake Off*. "A date?"

I'd been reflecting on how chill it was just to sit with him and be like a normal couple.

"Yeah, you know, like a date."

"I don't really...do dates." Gage put his book down and looked at me. "But you want me to, so I guess I will. Because I'm weak for you."

I leaned in to kiss his cheek. "Yeah, you are."

The next night we went to a movie together.

I dressed in designer jeans and one of the fancy button downs Gage had bought me.

Examining myself in the mirror, I was looking better. The bruises and marks had all but faded and although I'd lost a lot of weight in the cage I was almost back to where I was before then.

I washed my face and styled my hair and felt pretty damn human. Almost like normal again. I knew I'd be tired by the end of the night, my energy levels were still replenishing but... I felt good.

Gage's face lit up when he saw me which made my heart flutter.

"You look great." He pulled me in by the waist.

I wrapped my arms around his neck and we kissed. My heart fluttered even more and my dick started to harden just from the proximity and the scent of him. I pulled back.

"Maybe we don't have to go out?" I traced a line down his chest with one finger.

Gage shook his head. "No, you wanted a date and I'm going to give you a date. A fucking romantic night out, because you deserve to be wooed."

"Oh my god."

Gage shook a finger in my face. "You wanted this! You're getting my woo game tonight."

He picked up a jacket and held it out for me to put on.

"Please never say woo game again."

"No promises."

I slipped my arms into the jacket and he slid it smoothly up to my shoulders and patted me down. "How are you the worst and the best at the same time?"

"Oh, I've always been that. Even before I was turned, I'm just talented."

Gage kissed my cheek and offered me his arm. I took it happily. "Very talented."

The movie wasn't the best I'd ever seen. The newest installment in the Jurassic Park franchise, it was satisfyingly stupid with lots of cool dinosaurs and far-fetched action sequences.

Gagepaid extra for the fancy recliner seats which meant we had the best possible view. He'd also paid for all the snacks and drinks I wanted, so I was well set up with popcorn, candy, an ice cream cone and a jumbo soda.

Once I'd finished my ice cream, he reached out to hold my hand. I felt like a kid with a crush. Even though we'd been together a while now, and we'd done all sorts of unspeakably erotic things, the hand-holding felt exciting and new.

Gage's thumb rubbed the back of my hand and I relaxed back into the seat.

I had been half concerned that a big loud action movie would spook me, but thankfully,Nothing there in it triggered anything. I was glad. I felt more stable than I'd been when we went to the convenience store and that was a pleasant thing to realize.

When the movie ended, Gage stood up and stretched his arms over his head.

I had almost nodded off in the final moments of the movie. I set my chair back to the upright position and yawned so large it made my jaw click.

Gage offered me his hand. "You want to go for ice cream, or for a drink or something?"

I shook my head. "Nah, I'm beat. Let's head home."

"Right you are."

He held my hand as he led me out of the aisle.

We were in the corridor heading towards the lobby when I caught sight of a shadowy figure lurking the corner.

I jumped, grabbing Gage's arm. I was sure it was a vampire, someone coming to attack us. To take me away again. "Gage!"

"What?"

He followed my line of sight. "That's the usher, he's gonna clean up the cinema."

I blinked. Yep, that was an ordinary teenager in a cinema uniform waiting with a broom and dustpan to clean up the place.

"Sorry." I breathed, more to the kid than to Gage.

Gage slipped his arm around me and walked me out to the parking lot. "You okay?"

"I feel stupid. That kid probably thinks I'm insane now."

"You're not insane, you're traumatized." Gage corrected. "And honestly? We're probably never going to see that kid again so what he thinks doesn't even matter."

I breathed out. My heart was still thudding but my head was clearer. "Yeah. Thanks."

Gage kissed my cheek and opened the passenger side door for me to step in. "No worries. Let's get you home."

The simple fact he was taking care of me made tears well in

my eyes, but I swiped them away. He'd been looking after me for weeks, it wasn't a new thing. Maybe it was just because my blood was up from the scare?

Gage played some chill music over the car stereo and when we got home we went straight to bed.

Gage molded himself against my back and spooned me until I fell asleep.

It was strange to be in bed with my smoking hot boyfriend and not mess around, but my body - and my mind — wasn't quite there yet.

――――――――

Finally, enough time had passed that I was ready for more than cuddling.

Gage sat down with me to watch some *Bake Off* . "Is *that* his finished cake? Pathetic, at this stage they should be plating better than that."

He slipped his arm around me and my entire libido sat up to attention.

I crawled into his lap.

He looked at me, bemused. "Hi?"

I rolled my hips, grinding on him. "Take me to bed?"

Gage stroked his hands down my sides, careful as anything. "Are you sure you're up to that?"

"Yes, definitely." I leaned in to kiss him, thinking it would emphasize my point. Gage had been generous with cuddles and kisses, reassuring strokes on the back and muscle massages but he had ruled out any sex stuff until I was fully healed.

"If you're sure. We won't do anything too rough, let's just...get to know each other's bodies first."

"Did you read that somewhere? Have you been reading up on trauma or something?"

"No duh, of course I have." He rolled his eyes. "You might

think you want something and then it turns out that it triggers you and then we're back at emotional square one."

"I'm fine." I rolled my hips again. "And I'd really, really like some light bondage. After all this, I want to feel like I'm yours again."

Gage groaned and tipped his head back. "We shouldn't. It's still too soon."

"My wounds are healed, I'm hydrated and fed, and I've rested for days and days. Weeks, even. You've been looking after me so well. I'm good for this, please, Sir?"

I put on my best puppy-dog pout and made my eyes as big as they'd go. He looked back and groaned again.

"As if I could say no to you."

He lifted me as he stood up.

I wrapped my arms and legs around him koala-style and kissed his neck as he carried me to the bedroom.

"We're using traffic lights again, got it?"

I nodded and licked his ear.

He shivered lightly and sat on the bed, not tossing me like he might have before the incident. Instead he wrapped his arms around me and kissed me hard.

I relished how close he was to me. How I could feel his cool skin even through his T-shirt. How my body responded to him with arousal and need, even though I'd been through so much.

I pressed as tight against him as I could get and hummed into the kiss. I wanted him, I wanted this, I wanted...

My mind went blank. Even as his cool hands gripped the hem of my T-shirt and tugged it up over my head, I couldn't think of what I wanted.

It didn't matter. Gage would take care of me. I trusted him, and I'd told him what I wanted. He always knew just what I needed, sometimes before I did.

Gage kissed my collarbone, his lips incredibly gentle,

feathering over my skin and making me shiver. I put my arms around his shoulders.

It felt weird to be so close to him and not feel the strength of his lust. There was something there, but it was butterfly-faint. I hadn't realized just how much I enjoyed the empathic link, how distanced I felt from him now that it wasn't as strong.

It must feel the same for him too, right?

I pulled him closer with my arms and pressed against him, trying to communicate my need, my desire in a physical way. Gage held me tight for a moment, and then rolled us over, so I was on my back on the bed. He went up on an elbow and studied my face.

"You sure you're okay?"

"Yeah."

"You're quieter than usual."

"It's... strange not feeling the link." I didn't want to lie to him. Not now, not ever. "I'm adjusting to that."

"I want to feel it too." Gage traced a line down my cheek with one finger. "But it would mean feeding and I need you to be back at full strength before I do that."

Feeding... I had loved it in the past.

The memory of it was clear. I'd begged for it. I'd come from it. But that was the distant past. My mind heard the word 'feeding' and coupled it instantly with 'livestock'. I shied away from it.

Gage blinked. I'd actually cringed back from his hand. "Sorry, I—"

"No. That is exactly why I don't want to do it."

I looked up at the ceiling suddenly close to tears. Guilt twisted my stomach and fear sped up my heart. "I know it's not the same. You never hurt me, never. But I still—"

"Don't try and explain, I get it." Gage leaned in and planted a kiss on my cheek. "Don't worry. I have a supply, I'm fine. Nothing before you're ready."

I scrubbed the back of my hand against my eyes. "I want to be ready. I want to erase everything that happened from my memory."

"Unfortunately, that's not how it works." Gage sounded amused, but sympathetic. "If I've learned anything, it's that you can't just ignore shit that's happened. Listen, we can stop. You know? If you'd rather just cuddle and talk, we can do that."

I considered it.

I felt fragile. Like a moth that might fly into a light and burn up, or like I might tear if he touched me the wrong way. But I meant what I'd said. I wanted to move on, and this was a step I needed to take.

"No, I want you. I do." I leaned up and kissed him, biting on his lower lip and tugging it. My dick had softened completely but now Gage ran a hand through my hair and pulled. I moaned, dick waking up again.

"Say it again, make me believe it." Gage's voice had dropped lower and my arousal heightened.

"Please, Master." I whispered it, unable to speak any louder than that. My heart pounded in my ears. "Please fuck me?"

"As you wish." Gage sat back to remove my pants and shuffle them down my legs.

He took his own clothes off next. I drank in the sight of him as his skin was revealed. I loved him so much. So smooth, so gorgeous, my slim vampire dom. I reached to touch him, a daring move that I usually wouldn't have tried. But this wasn't a usual evening, or a normal scene. Everything was new to us. The enormity of what had happened had given us a fresh start.

"Please." My voice was stronger this time. I lay flat back and raised my arms over my head, letting my hands fall loosely on the bed. I was confident that this was something he would respond to.

How could he not? I was offering myself up.

Gage smiled and leaned down, gathering my wrists together

and pinning them with one hand. "My gorgeous puppy." His free hand stroked down my side. "I'll give you anything you want."

He kissed me, harder this time, more like the old Gage. My body arched up off the bed to taste more of him.

"Such a good boy for me." Gage reached over to the drawer.

My excitement spiked. I'd asked for something light, what would he choose?

18

GAGE

Thank all the stars above that Brand couldn't feel how afraid
I was.

I was sure something I did would trigger a memory and he'd
curl in on himself and never come out again. I moved at a snail's
pace.

I should have refused outright, but Brand wanted it, and if
Brand wanted it I was going to give it to him. I'd give him
everything, the moon, my apartment, my car. Anything. If he
wanted this well, I'd give it to him— but I'd be careful about it.

The memory of how he'd looked in that basement was
etched onto my mind. Although I knew he was doing better now,
I saw grayness still lingering at the edges of him. The bags under
his eyes, his thin cheeks. He wasn't back to where he'd been
before.

So.

Careful.

Instead of his leather cuffs (too sturdy) or anything metal
(too reminiscent of the cage) I pulled out a handful of black silk
scarves. I'd used them on him before. The night we played the
'Can you get away?' game. I had tied them loosely then, and the
temptation to do that again was strong.

He looked up at me with those gorgeous brown eyes, pools of longing.

I shouldn't cheat him of this. I was responsible for giving him what he asked for, what he needed.

I wrapped the silk around his wrists, looping it twice before tying it off, not too tight but enough to hold him if he didn't struggle.

It wasn't a lot, but it was enough to get me deeply aroused, to see him laid out and bound for me, wanting me to do whatever I liked to him.

"How's that?" I leaned in to kiss the corner of his mouth.

He squirmed under me, flushing. "Yeah."

"Hitch your knees up."

He did it, obedient boy. I spread his ankles wide, holding them in place before I leaned in to eat him out.

He always whined so deliciously when I did this and tonight was no exception.

"Master..." His voice broke into a whine part way through the word. I stroked a hand over his thigh and circled his hole with my tongue.

My goals for the evening were simple: give him pleasure, but don't overwhelm him. If I really got him going he might get overstimulated and fall apart. He might close off, or go too deep and hurt himself somehow, psychologically.

I really ought to read up more on trauma survivors and coping mechanisms.

Now wasn't the time.

I pushed my tongue into him. Brand shuddered, his thighs pressing in against my shoulders and his body lifting ever so slightly off the bed for a second. If I had been able to, I'd have smirked. I loved how responsive he was. Having such a warm and sensitive pet went to my head.

I worked him over, taking my time to tease him open, letting him really feel it and relax into it. I wouldn't be rough with him tonight, wasn't capable of it even if I wanted to. He needed coddling, he needed to be fussed over, and I was more than happy to do just that.

His whines turned into soft begging, his voice hardly more than a murmur.

"Master... Master please I need more, please..."

I lubed my finger and pushed it inside, circling it slowly then reaching to prod gently at his prostate. He moaned with something like relief. He tensed around me and then loosened even more. I repeated the movement, moving my head up to lick the precum off the head of his dick.

"You like that?"

It was a tease of a question, something both of us knew the answer to, being made to say it out loud would arouse him.

"Y-yeah, love it."

I pressed one more time. "You ready for me, do you think?"

That was a question I never asked. I was good at reading his responses, feeling his need, gauging the readiness of his body, but tonight was different. I wanted him to feel as in control as possible.

"Yes! Please, yes Master, I'm ready for you to fuck me."

"Such a dirty mouth." I couldn't resist taking him fully into my mouth for a moment. He was slick with saliva and lubed and ready.

"Check in, Brand."

"Green."

"Good boy."

I got into position, circled his hole once more with my thumb before lubing myself and pushing inside.

He was so tight, tight as if I'd never fucked him before.

I wrapped an arm around his waist and leaned on the elbow of the other arm, my concerns for Brand vanishing as I enjoyed how good he felt. I loved having him spread out below me. He loved to be mine.

I kissed him, harder than I had in days, fuelled by my own need for him.

He returned it hungrily, moaning and panting into my mouth, messy and hot.

I pumped my hips, not wanting to go too fast or too rough, but needing to feel the motion of it.

He responded, his own hips rocking in time with mine.

I pulled back from the kiss, breathless myself although I hardly needed to breathe. "Check in."

"G-green." He gasped, craning his neck to kiss me again.

I obliged him happily, exploring his mouth with mine and pushing him back down into the pillows.

I pulled him closer against me, speeding up. Maybe this would be all right? Maybe the crash and burn I'd been fearing wouldn't happen.

I relaxed, enjoying myself more thoroughly, kissing his jaw and then down his throat, the way I'd done a hundred times before.

That was when it all went to shit.

19

BRANDON

Green. I'd said green.

I'd meant green. I *was* green.

Until his lips found my throat.

My body tensed. Terror filled me and I flinched back from him.

Suddenly I couldn't stand the thought of being bound, even with the flimsiest of scarves. I yanked my hands in different directions, breathing only when the silk came free.

One hand went to my own neck, feeling for a wound that logically I knew wasn't there. He hadn't bitten me, had barely even kissed me, but my heart thundered. Everything in my brain screamed DANGER

Gage pulled back instantly, slipping out of me, his eyes wide. "Brand, what's going on?"

"Stop, I need to stop." My mind flooded with words but there were only two right ones. "Red! Red, uh, seasalt, okay?"

"Yeah, of course." Gage sat back on his heels, one hand stroking my thigh, his face a picture of concern. "Just tell me what you need."

What did I need? I needed to be safe.

A second ago I'd felt safe. I was with Gage and Gage would

never abuse me. We'd played with pain before, and I knew I liked his bites but... no.

Everything in me said no. I wrapped my arms around myself and screwed my eyes shut. I was going to cry. Fuck, I was going to cry in the middle of having sex with my wonderful boyfriend.

Sex that I'd begged for.

Hot tears leaked out from between my lashes. I felt horribly guilty. None of this was his fault. He didn't hurt me, he'd been nothing but kind to me, but all I could think of was the pain Shawna and Ford had caused me.

"Shit. Brand. I'm so sorry." He moved closer. I felt the mattress sink, but he didn't touch me. "I'm so sorry. Can I hold you?"

I considered this.. I wanted to be held, wanted to be comforted — but he was the same kind of monster Shawna was. Had been. He wanted to suck my blood, too. My muscles tensed and the primal, lizard part of my brain screamed RUN! Predator!

I twitched back from him.

"Brand? Please breathe? I don't think you're..."

I sucked in a huge breath. Some of the ache in my chest vanished. My chest was aching? When had that started? I breathed out slowly, trying to get some semblance of control over myself.

Gage pulled the blanket up over me, moved in beside me and tentatively touched my hip.

I flinched back further, hating myself for doing it.

"I'm sorry," I gasped. "It's not you. It's—"

"Yeah."

I took another few breaths, slow and deliberate. My head cleared a little. My eyes were still streaming tears and my nose was stuffed up, but I felt more myself. I'd resisted the urge to flee, which I figured was a good thing.

Slowly I realized that Gage's presence behind me was a comfort, so I rolled over and pressed against his chest.

"Hold me?" My voice was so strangled, so high and thin I hardly recognized it.

Gage moved slowly, winding his arms around me and holding on loosely, so if I panicked again I could easily break free. But this was what I needed. I leaned my face into him and inhaled, reassuring myself with his scent.

"You're shaking, baby. Just keep breathing okay? I've got you. Nothing bad's gonna happen. I'll keep you safe. I'll protect you."

I was sobbing now, his words bringing out my fears in a way I hadn't been able to express out loud. I longed for the connection between us. To feel what he was feeling, that was the comfort I needed.

But to get that... he'd have to feed off me. Every fiber of my body said NO to that.

Probably for the best the empathic link was all but broken. I was glad Gage didn't have to feel the jumble of fear, guilt, longing, sadness and devotion I was experiencing.

I'm sure he could tell enough from my reactions.

"Take your time." Gage kissed the top of my head. "I'm not going anywhere. You let it all out and take your time. There's no rush, we have all the time in the world. Whatever you need, I'll give it to you, okay?"

Gage's words unlocked something inside. I sobbed out my fears and pain until I ran out of tears. Then he helped me to blow my nose and pull on pajama pants. No more sex tonight.

He gave me a drink of water, and then a sports drink for the electrolytes lost, and we sat side by side against the pillows while I pulled myself together.

Finally, I spoke. "I'm sorry."

"Don't apologize." Gage squeezed my hand. "You've been through a fucking nightmare, of course you're going to have moments where you lose it. Anyone would."

I sighed and squeezed his hand back.

"Well, I'm sorry it happened like that. When it did."

"I wasn't going to bite you, we talked about that."

"I know. I know we did, and I know you wouldn't have. But my body didn't know. It went right back to the cage."

Gage let go of my hand to lift his arm up. "Thanks for using the safe word."

I snuggled in against him. "Weird thing to thank me for. I ruined our evening."

"No." Gage squeezed me against him for a brief moment. "If you're not into it, then I don't want to be doing it. You're too precious for that. I wanted you to feel in control and you used your word. That was the best thing you could have done."

I felt a wave of relief. "Are you sure?"

"Brand, that's why we have them. I'm sure. I love you, you know? I want you to be happy, as happy as you can be. If you're not happy, I want to know about it."

I nodded, pressing a kiss into his chest.

We sat like that for a while. Him holding me, solid as a rock, me slowly getting my heart rate back to normal, the shivers easing off.

Finally, I yawned.

"Come on, let's get you to sleep," he said.

"I just wanted..." I sighed and rubbed my face. "I wanted to feel something really good again."

"You were enjoying it quite a lot for a while there."

"Yeah but we didn't—"

Gage interrupted me. "You got some pleasure out of it, right? That's what counts. There's lots of kinds of sex after all."

"But I didn't even come, and you didn't either."

"So?" Gage gathered me back into his arms. "I got to be with you, touch you, make you moan. I like that."

I chewed on this idea and then nodded. "Okay. Yeah, I liked it too."

"Maybe going forward, we'll just take things real slow. Try

one new thing at a time and see what works. How does that sound?"

I kissed him, flooded with happiness and a small amount of relief. "Yes, that's perfect."

He kissed me back and then laid me down on the bed, pulling the blankets up around us both. "For now though, sleep. Okay, puppy?"

"Yeah. Sounds good." I closed my eyes. It had been a rollercoaster, I felt wrung out and rattled, but ultimately, thanks to Gage's patience and his kind words, I felt safe again. He held me as I fell asleep.

20

BRANDON

Weeks passed. I went back to classes at school. I moved more of my things into Gage's apartment. Between us we worked up to full sex and some spankings, but no biting. I just couldn't go there, even though I knew it wouldn't be painful, that it would actually be a wonderful experience. It was too much.

Martina had gone back to Washington, but she texted every day and called every few days.

Max and I had lunch most days, and he took me to the beach to surf a couple of times.

Probably the most important development was Gage paying for me to see a trauma therapist.

I wasn't sure about her going in. I didn't mind talking to Gage about it, but he insisted I see someone who for sure knew what they were doing.

Getting started was hard, but our first session put me at ease. She was kind and patient, asking all sorts of easy questions about my life, my family, my friends and so on. 'Getting your context' she called it.

After that I didn't mind talking through the experiences I'd had. There was a lot I had to talk around, since she obviously wasn't aware of the existence of vampires. Ultimately it didn't matter. She taught me breathing exercises, how to recognize when I was spiraling and some useful ways to reframe things.

I started to meditate, which was something she thought I probably did unconsciously when I surfed. Although it felt awkward to start with, I ended up being pretty good about it.

As the days and weeks passed, I felt more and more myself.

I was headed back to Gage's after my last Friday class when he called me.

"Hey."

"Hey, Brand. I'm gonna head to Club V and catch up with Athena. Do you want to come?"

I blinked. An unexpected bonus to all of this was Gage had connected with the local vampire community. The decent ones.

He'd told me Club V was where I'd been held, but to me it was just some basement. I had no memory of the club itself, having never seen it. My heart sped up at the idea of being around other vampires. But Gage would be there, and Athena had been so angry at her space being abused she'd added a whole lot of security and extra cameras and so on to be sure it could never happen again.

She'd even sent me an apology bouquet to the hospital.

"Sure...yeah."

"Only if you're sure. The second you feel uncomfortable we can leave."

"No, I'm sure, I want to meet her." He'd been texting Athena and a few others regularly. Montague, the leather worker, had heard about what happened and been in touch with Gage as well to ask if there was anything he could do.

I wanted Gage to have a community, and I was curious as hell about what happened at a vampire club.

"Okay, so we'll go when you get back. Their Friday nights can get kinda raucous, she said, but we'll be there while it's quiet and hopefully not overwhelming."

"I'm excited," I said, meaning it. "I'll be back there in ten."

"I'll find something for you to change into."

Gage hung up as I told him off for judging what I was wearing when he was the one who had bought it all for me.

Something had changed in our dynamic and I expected it was for the better. It wasn't just him being all dommy and me doing what I was told. We were on more equal footing now. It felt more like a normal relationship.

As normal as dating a vampire could ever be.

I felt confident. I didn't jump at shadows and I was only half-paranoid when I thought someone might be following me.

At the apartment, Gage had laid out tight black jeans, a soft black short sleeved shirt and my collar on the bed. I eyed the selection and considered how I felt about it.

"The collar is a suggestion, only!" he called out. I looked over to see him in the en suite.

He was fussing with his hair, which he'd started growing out at some stage in the last month. No longer shaving the sides, it looked sort of ragged. It was pale roots and bright red tips. He noticed me looking.

"I think I might dye it black, what do you think?"

"I think you'll look cool whatever you do." I leaned in the doorway. He was dressed in all black as well, we were going to match. Surprisingly cute.

"Not helpful." He sprayed a generous amount of mousse into his hand and styled his hair into something like a pompadour. "It's been forever since I did something like this."

"Dyed your hair?" I teased.

He glared at me in the mirror. "Other vampires, Friday night, Club."

I slipped my arms around his neck and smiled at his reflection. "Like you said if either of us gets uncomfortable we can just leave."

He leaned back a bit in my arms. "Yeah."

"So what's the deal with you being able to see yourself in a mirror?" I asked.

Gage rolled his eyes. "Beats me. I'm glad I can though. I read a theory that it was something to do with silver backings that they don't use on mirrors anymore, but who the fuck knows."

I made a mental note to ask around if I ever became friends with the other vampires too.

"I'll wear the collar. I like the idea of everyone looking at us and knowing I'm yours."

Gage grabbed my hand and squeezed. "Cause you are. And I'm yours."

"Damn right." I hesitated to kiss the product-filled top of his head, so I leaned awkwardly over.

He tilted his head back and we did an upside-down spiderman kiss. "Now go get changed, I want to get there."

"Bossy."

"You love it."

I let go of him and stripped as I walked back into the bedroom. I could feel his eyes on me like a ray of sunshine.

21

GAGE

I felt like a kid on the first day of school.
Or like I was about to be naked on stage with nothing to say.
I was a fucking vampire, I shouldn't be intimidated by this.
But here we were, pulling up at the valet parking for Club V and
I wanted to bail.
Brand was wide-eyed and bouncing in his seat.
We got out of the car. I handed the human valet my keys and
a twenty. "Somewhere easy to get to, we won't be staying too
long."
"Understood, sir." He gave me a bow and climbed into
the car.
I took Brand by the arm and we walked into the place
together. The foyer looked much the same as the last time I'd
seen it, although the bar was visibly busier.
Athena was at the front desk with a young human woman in
full rockabilly pin-up gear. They both looked up and smiled
at us.
"Fifi this is Gage, and his boyfriend Brand. We're going to be
seeing a lot of them from now on." Athena said, confidently.
"They have platinum access."
Fifi grinned wide. "Nice to meet you both."

"Sorry if this is rude to ask, but is Fifi your real name?" Brand asked.

She giggled. "Fiona, but that's so predictable."

Brand chuckled. I was glad to hear that sound.

"Wait, what's platinum access?"

"Come on and sit and I'll tell you all about it." Athena led us through to the bar and sat us at a booth with a decent amount of light and a view of the stage. The stage was currently empty, but I expected the shows didn't start until later in the evening. "Now, what can I get you?"

"Whatever you have is fine." She'd know I meant blood.

"Just a coke," Brand said.

"Nonsense, you must be hungry too. I'll get you a platter." She went to place the order at the bar and then sat opposite us.

"It's good to see you." Athena leaned towards Brand. "You look a lot better than when I last saw you."

"Thanks, I'm feeling a lot better."

Brand's smile was slightly strained, so I changed the subject. "What's platinum?"

"A membership level, the highest we have. We can set aside a room for your exclusive use, and if you let us know in advance we can keep this booth free for you. Drinks on the house and discounts on food."

"You don't have to do all that." I shook my head. "I can pay."

"I'm sure you can but at this place, you won't. I feel dreadful about what happened, and I'm not going to hear another word about it. You're honored guests any time you visit."

"Cool." Brand grinned.

I relaxed back against the booth as a waiter brought a tray of drinks and a loaded platter of food for Brand. It was a charcuterie board with various cold cuts and cheeses, little pots of pickled things and cakes as well. Brand dug in immediately. I watched him fondly, only looking up when Athena cleared her throat.

"So, how have you been?"

"Good," I said. "You?"

"Good." She laughed some. "I liked that movie you recommended."

"You recommended a movie?" Brand looked between us, a hunk of cheese speared on a fork halfway to his mouth.

"Only Lovers Left Alive," I said. "We watched it together, remember?"

"Your obsession with vampire movies." Brand rolled his eyes.

"Obviously it's no Lost Boys, the best vampire movie in history, but I liked it."

"It was fun. I've been playing some of the soundtrack at the club." Athena leaned on her elbow and propped her chin on her hand. "By the by, we have a play night coming up, if you're interested."

I glanced at Brand who was now thoroughly riveted by the food in front of him. "Maybe. Maybe just to watch."

"Whatever you like, I'll text you the details." She winked at me. "It's good to see you out. Our kind aren't meant to be solitary you know."

I sighed and sipped my drink, a gently warmed O positive. "Yeah. I'm getting that. When everything went wrong..." I glanced again at Brand. He was studying the platter with a look that told me he was listening hard but pretending not to. "I had no one to call. It sucked ass and I don't ever want to feel that alone again."

"Community is important to all of us. Here you have a family, if you want it." Athena's expression was serious. She wanted me to respond.

Beside me, Brand moved closer, pressing his thigh against mine. The faintest of emotions came through our empathic link, possibly heightened by the physical touch. Brand's feeling was all warm and affection. A yes if ever I felt it.

"It's not easy for me to trust." I reached for Brand's hand.

"After my sire... and then what I knew of the vampire community was all..." Words didn't seem adequate for my disgust and hurt, so I stuck my tongue out. "It sucked. It was easier for me to be on my own. But... I don't want to be any more."

"You're not alone." Brand's voice was soft.

"That's right." Athena's gaze hadn't left my face. Her expression was soft, eyebrows together, all compassion. "You have Brand and all of us here at V. I interviewed everyone and no one knew the basement was being used by those low-lifes. You can trust everyone on my staff."

I chewed my lower lip, wanting to believe it, and finding resistance even still.

"You shared your sire with Shawna and Ford, isn't that right?" Athena prodded gently.

"You did?" Brand's eyes widened.

"Yeah. I guess you were out of it for that whole revelation." I squeezed his hand and leaned back against the booth, looking up at the ceiling. My emotions swirled. Anger, first and foremost, but I could also remember how much it hurt.

Rufus had courted me, convinced me how wonderful it would all be. He'd made me think he cared, and then, once he'd turned me, he lost interest.

In hours he was onto the next target. He barely even told me what I needed to know to survive and let me loose on the night.

"Rufus is an asshole. I'm not surprised he turned those two. He's... I haven't seen him since I dunno, 1995? He doesn't care about the ones he's sired. He just likes the hunt, the game of it all. Convincing pretty kids that he has something they need, and then when they succumb to him he's onto the next one."

Athena drummed her fingernails on the table, I forced my chin down to look at her. "There are rules against that."

"Yeah well, no one's enforcing them so it doesn't count for shit."

She made a face like she'd sucked on a lemon. "I'll talk to the magistrate. Maybe there's something that can be done."

"Magistrate? Are there vampire... cops?" Brand was enthralled.

I chuckled, looking at his wide-eyed wonder.

"There have to be." Athena had her phone in her hand and was tapping rapidly. "I'll see if I can get hold of her. For now, I'll leave you guys to it. Feel free to wander around, look anywhere." Her eyes flicked up to Brand. "The basement has been cleaned out and renovated. It's a quiet lounge area now, just... in case you'd like to see it."

Brand shook his head. "Nope."

"Probably for the best. Thanks, Athena, for everything." She waved the thanks off as she moved away, engrossed in her phone.

"She's so cool." Brand leaned against me until I slipped my arm around him.

"Not cooler than me, I hope." I said it lightly, teasing but I was secretly worried that more exposure to the world of vampires might make Brand rethink his decision to be with me.

"Oh way cooler."

My heart sank.

"But I dunno man, she's always on her phone. I prefer someone more hands on." He turned his face to mine so I could see his cheeky grin.

I gave him a relieved kiss.

"Hands on is something I'm very good at."

"I know."

Brand's expression became more serious. "I'm sorry about your sire."

I shrugged, jostling him with the movement. "I mean, yeah, it sucks but I'm used to it, you know."

"I get that."

"So, how are you feeling, do you want to head back home?"

Brand shook his head. "I want to look around more. See what kind of facilities are on offer."

I chuckled. "You make it sound like a gym we're interested in joining."

Brand laughed. "It's not entirely different is it?"

We got up. Brand stretched his shoulders, enough that his shirt rode up to show a tantalizing strip of abs. I tugged him close and kissed him again. He responded beautifully, melting against me. The atmosphere of the place seemed to be having a positive effect on him.

The club was quiet, a few people at the bar and not much else as we started to walk around. The mezzanine was occupied now. Two gorgeous people sat on huge armchairs and sipped on cocktails, talking to each other. One was a man, one was a woman, and they both looked like they were out of a fashion magazine.

"Who are they?" Brand asked.

"Blood for hire," I said. "Vampires pay a fair bit of money for some alone time to drink from them."

Brand was silent for a moment.

Had I triggered something? I glanced around, homing in on the closest exit.

"That's a really good idea," he said, finally. "They're consenting, and that way a vampire isn't out like hunting or whatever."

Relieved, I wrapped my arm tighter around him. "Yeah. From what Athena told me they have full right of refusal, and there's a bodyguard watching at all times."

"Alone time is a euphemism then?"

"Exactly. I bet after recent events there are even more security measures in place." We walked on. "Down here are the playrooms, do you want to have a look?"

"Does the pope shit in the woods?"

"I don't think he does, actually."

Brand laughed. "Right, probably not, but I do want to look at the rooms."

I let Brand lead the way. All the doors stood slightly ajar to show they weren't in use. For the most part they had the same design and were stocked with the same equipment. A St Andrew's cross, a leather bench, a wall which held a small supply of whips, crops, paddles and cuffs, and a large couch for aftercare. The ceilings had hooks and pulley systems for suspension play and most rooms had either a swing or a pole.

Each room smelled of cleaning products and leather polish.

Towards the far end of the hallway there were larger, more specialized rooms. There was a neon graffiti decorated room that reminded me of punk clubs from the eighties. A modern one which had fake windows that showed a cityscape, and some superhero decals on the walls. There was a lush Marseilles inspired room with a huge four-poster bed and lots of mirrors. Brand lingered at the superhero room but turned up his nose at the French luxury.

The next room was hardcore with a hard wooden bed with riveted cuffs attached, a set of steel stocks and a human-sized cage in the corner.

Brand had pushed the door open to look inside but pressed back against me swiftly. "Not that room."

I wrapped my arms around him and directed him to the next one. "No, never that room."

The next one had him relaxing in my arms. It was dominated by a large four poster bed with a set of leather-lined stocks built into the foot end.

A large rack leaned against the wall, but it was a padded leather one that looked almost inviting, along with a huge sectional couch and a built-in mirror on the far wall. The decor was classic; deep red walls and black furniture. It was probably my favorite of the rooms as well.

"I could play here." Brand walked a couple of steps inside.

"Now?" I asked, surprised.

"Well... maybe not right now." Brand's expression was hopeful. "But soon?"

I kissed him, elated. "Absolutely. The moment you're ready to."

He wrapped his arms around my waist and kissed me again. "But... maybe we could go home and play there?"

"Maybe we could. Is that how pets ask their Masters for things?"

Brand pulled away and sank to his knees, looking up at me with big eyes and holding his hands in front of him like a puppy begging. "Please, Master, will you take me home and play with me?"

The sight had me instantly hard.

"Fuck." I grabbed his collar by the ring in front and yanked him in to nuzzle against my crotch, so he could feel the effect he had on me through my pants.

He mouthed at me through the fabric.

"You sure you don't want to stay and use this room?"

Brand pulled himself back from my pants with a visible effort. "No, I'm not sure. Can we use this room?"

"Athena said we could use whatever we wanted. Just... be aware when we're done the club will probably be busier and you might see like, some feeding or whatever."

Brand considered this, sitting back on his heels, hands on his knees.

"Let's do it."

"Okay. I think I just..." I turned to the keypad on the outside of the door. "Athena texted me a code." I tapped the numbers into the pad and the little display said, 'Welcome Gage. 60 minutes remaining.'

"Very cool."

I pulled the door closed behind me and licked my lips. One thing to sort out before we started. "There's a window here, all the rooms have them. We can leave the blind open so people can watch or we can close it for privacy. Up to you."

"Close it," Brand said. "But maybe next time we're here, we leave it open."

"Sounds good to me." I closed the blind and shrugged off my shirt, hanging it on a convenient hook. "Tell me your safeword."

Brand rolled his eyes. "Seasalt, and the colors are green for yes, I'm good, orange for slow down and red for stop."

"What's with this sass?" I swaggered closer to him, letting my eyes narrow. "Are you going to be a brat for me tonight?"

Brand licked his lips. For the first time in weeks, he looked like the old Brand. "Maybe." The glimpse of his tongue had my dick pulsing.

He'd never been much of a brat for me, always happy to kneel and do what he was told.Was this the start of something new for us?

I went to the wall of supplies and grabbed a leather leash, clipping it to his collar and tugging him back into my crotch for more nuzzling.

"If you want this, babe, you have to be a good boy."

Brand groaned, his hands instantly on my thighs, kneading. He moved his open mouth up and down my dick, wetting the fabric of my pants.

"Answer me."

22

BRANDON

"Answer me."

I didn't. I just kept working my mouth over the hardness of him and moaning.

I wasn't sure what had come over me. My need to be good for him, to be a good pet and please him was nowhere to be found. I felt playful and naughty. Those feelings made me want to laugh out loud.

I hadn't felt this bubbly and fun since before the whole kidnapping thing and I was determined to ride this high.

Gage yanked me back by the leash, briefly choking me so I sputtered. My dick was so hard it ached against the tight denim.

"I said, answer me."

I looked up at him, playing innocent. "What was the question?"

"Are you going to be a good boy?"

I tilted my head to the side, pretending to consider this. "I don't know, are you going to give me a reason to?"

Gage growled, a low noise full of promise. "Oh I see. Gonna test me, aren't you?"

My skin tingled at the sound and the look in his eye. He was pleased, maybe as excited as I was, but he was playing his role.

"This way then." He walked towards the padded leather rack, holding tight to my leash. I had to scramble to follow. He paused, looking at me as I stood up.

"Crawl. Be a good dog and crawl for me."

I flushed. My desire to play up faded at the thought of humiliating myself by crawling behind him like a dog. It was still a playful thing to do, I reasoned. I dropped to all fours and followed him that way.

"That's my good boy."

His words went right through me. I didn't really want to misbehave did I? I wanted to be a good boy.

But the playful energy was still in me. He could have this, but I'd make it difficult for him some other way.

He tugged me up while standing. "Undress."

My hands went to the buttons on my shirt and I started to undo them, but painfully slowly. It was a stark contrast to how quickly I usually obeyed.

Gage huffed through his nose. "Puppy…"

"What?" I looked down at him.

"If you don't start moving faster I'm going to tear that shirt off you."

I barely stifled a moan. I wanted him to tear my clothes off, wanted to feel that desperation from him, but not here. Not when I'd have to walk out with no shirt if he did that, after we were done.

I got my shirt off and tossed it to the floor, going to undo my pants and slowing down again.

"Fuck it."

Gage was on me in a moment, his hands around my wrists, pushing me towards the leather bench. He pressed me against it and kissed me hard, biting gently on my lower lip. My hips bucked against his.

I wanted more. I didn't want him to be gentle the way he had been for the last few weeks. I wanted the old Gage.

He flipped me onto my front and made quick work of securing my wrists to the legs of the bench, stretching me out over the thing so my back and ass were exposed.

"Please," I breathed.

"Please, what?"

"Please, Master, I want more."

Gage snorted. "If you wanted to ask for things you should have been a good boy from the start."

He ran his hands over my back and then up my arms, fastening another set of cuffs above my elbows. I tugged against them and moaned.

"I'm sorry."

"I bet you are. But now I've got you right where I want you."

I moaned, trying to rut against the bench to get some friction. Gage caught my hips, undid my pants and had them off in a moment.

"I'm going to spank you for being naughty. Got that pup? If you're good and you count for me, maybe I'll give you what you want. But you have to be good, and you have to ask me nicely. Got that?"

"I, yeah. I mean, yes, Master."

He slapped my ass with the palm of his hand, making me jump. "That's what I like to hear."

I watched as he went back to the wall with all the whips. He ran his hand over a few items. When he paused at the riding crop, I moaned without meaning to.

He glanced at me, mouth pulling into a smirk. "You like this one, do you?"

Breathless, I nodded. "Yes, sir."

"Then I'll be kind and give you what you like."

The riding crop was one of my favorite impact tools. He'd used his own on me before and it was the perfect blend of sharp sting and no lasting pain. I rolled my hips in anticipation.

Gage took up a position beside me so I could see him if I

152

turned my head. He placed his hand in the center of my back and whipped the riding crop down.

The pain was heavenly. A sharp strike that had all my senses on alert, and the sting that melted into pleasure. I moaned loudly.

Gage's hand found my chin and he squeezed it. "Count for me."

I'd totally forgotten about that order, so into the idea of the crop. I hadn't even meant to misbehave.

"One, Master."

He brought it down again.

"Two, thank you Master."

Gage purred and stroked his hand over my ass. "There's my good boy."

He struck me again.

I jolted. He'd hit the exact same place twice in a row and the pain was sharper. I inhaled. "Three, thank you Master."

"Check in, Brand."

"Green."

He stroked my dick twice, making me moan louder.

He brought the crop down again a few more times. I just managed to keep count.

Finally he set the crop down and undid the cuffs. I could barely hold myself up, I was so gone on the pain and the pleasure. He gathered me into his arms and carried me to the bed, laying me down on the bed on my back.

I winced as my red-hot ass hit the bed.

"You good?"

"Yeah. Hurts in a good way." I reached to wrap my arms around him and pull him in for a kiss. I wanted him so badly it ached.

Gage climbed on top of me, grinding down as he kissed me back. One hand found the leash and tugged on it gently enough to remind me I still wore his collar.

I groaned, arching against him.

I wanted... everything.

My heart pounded in my ears, but I knew it was true, I wanted it. I was ready.

"Gage, Master... I want you to bite me, please."

Gage went still and pulled back enough to look me in the eye. "You're sure?"

I nodded, holding his gaze. "I'm sure. I'm ready, I want it. Not the neck maybe, but ... my wrist? My arm? Please, I want to feel you in every way possible. I want to be yours again, to feel how much you want me."

Gage hesitated, looking around at the room as if the answer would be written on the wall.

I reached for his cheek and gently turned him back to face me.

"I feel safe. I trust you, or I wouldn't have asked."

Gage's expression softened. He looked deep into me for a few long seconds.

"Okay. But I'm not going to tie you down while I do it."

I whined, wanting it, wanting everything.

Gage shook his head. "No. For this time, I want you to feel you're not helpless. But I know how much you love being tied up for me. So, how about this?" He lifted his hand and wound the leash around one of the bars in the headboard.

I tugged against it experimentally, felt the resistance and moaned softly.

I sank back into the pillows, aroused and nervous and absolutely, sickeningly in love.

"Yes, Daddy."

Gage stopped moving again. "What did you just call me?"

I flushed. It had just slipped out without my even thinking. I'd never called him Daddy before and I had no idea if he liked it or not. "I... sorry, Master, I didn't mean to, it just—"

Gage rolled his hips against mine. "You can call me that. But I'm not gonna do ageplay stuff."

I shook my head. "No, I don't want ageplay. It's just... you're hot and you're looking after me and it's just a bit... Daddy."

"I like it. For this context." He leaned in and kissed me, hot and hard.

I melted and my legs spread wide.

"Do you want fucking?" he reached down to stroke me. "Or just this?"

I groaned, pulling him in closer again. "Fuck me, please Daddy."

Gage kissed my jaw. "That's my good boy."

He grabbed a packet of lube from the side table and lubed his hand generously before starting to tease me open.

I thought briefly about the night I'd freaked out and safeworded, but as I looked at Gage, and touched him (touched him! That hardly ever happened while we fucked) I didn't feel anything but loved. He had bound my collar to the headboard, but he was ready to pull back the second I said the word.

I wouldn't. Not tonight. Warmth and yearning for him built as he teased me. Even though I might freak out a little afterwards, I wanted him to feed from me. I wanted our connection back, more than anything in the world.

My therapist had given me ways to cope and to frame the things that panicked me, and I was ready to use them.

Gage looked up and I cupped his cheek, moaning and gasping as he stretched me. A weird juxtaposition — him prepping me for sex and me feeling utterly soft and fond for him in the same moment.

Or maybe that's how it was supposed to be?

His eyes were dark, hungry, but he kissed my palm gently. "You good?"

"Yeah. Fantastic."

Once I was stretched, he moved above me, lining himself up

and pushing slowly into me. I moaned, arching my back. Gage grabbed my wrists and pinned them either side of my head, his fingers threaded with mine. He looked deep into my eyes.

"You're my everything."

I gasped, and he fitted his mouth over mine in a consuming kiss. I closed my eyes and rocked my hips, losing my mind with lust and love both.

"My hero." I gasped. "You saved me."

He shoved his hips harder into me. "No one will ever touch you but me, ever again." He mouthed over my jaw. "You're mine. Mine forever."

"Yes, Gage. Yes, Master, I'm yours. All yours."

"Mind, body and soul." Gage whispered, his lips tickling the skin below my earlobe. He was getting closer to my neck.

I bucked my hips, encouraging him to move more. "Please, Master." My voice came out strangled as Gage bucked his hips, hitting my prostate square on. A lump in my throat formed. I wanted him to bite, but I was nervous as well.

"What do you want, pet? Use your words."

"Please bite me."

"You said not the neck."

"I said maybe. It's okay, please bite my neck."

Gage hesitated, his lips feathering against my skin. I knew he was second-guessing if this was a good idea. He let go of one of my hands, but I left it resting on the bed. His fangs were out, I'd seen them.

"You're sure?" his voice was barely more than a whisper.

I tilted my head up, arching my throat for him. Some of it was covered by the leather collar of course, but it was a clear offer.

"I'm sure. Please Gage. I want to feel you in every way."

Gage bit into me without any further hesitation.

My heart raced. This bite was nothing like the bites Shawna and Ford had taken from me. Gage's fangs sunk into me smooth as butter with a slight sting and nothing else.

My body flooded with endorphins and my eyes teared up.

"Yes." I wrapped my free hand around his waist, pulling him closer again.

His hips bucked erratically.

He drank my blood and I felt whole.

Memories of when he'd fed from me previously flooded my mind. How good it felt, the feeling of being connected to him on the cellular level.

Gage pulled back too soon, licking over the wound and wrapping his arm around me to fuck me deep into the bed. He let go of my other hand to reach between us and pump my dick.

"Fuck you taste good." His voice rasped. "Come for me, pet."

I didn't need any more encouragement than his permission and the bite I'd requested. My body tensed and then released with the power of it. I cried out, closing my eyes and bucking against him.

Gage groaned and filled me, his mouth sliding down from the place he bit to my shoulder. "Love you so much."

"Love you."

Gage pulled out and kissed me again. He stroked my face and then undid the leash from my collar.

"How are you feeling?"

I hadn't let go of him and I didn't intend to. My body was shaky, partly from the sex but partly from the enormity of what had just happened. I had been bitten, and I was still okay.

"I'm..." I took a breath, trying to understand what was happening. "Fragile? I think... okay but a little unsure."

"Gotcha." Gage cuddled me closer to him and nuzzled his cheek to mine. "Take your time."

We lay like that for a while, him just holding me, me considering the emotions as they ran through me.

Finally, I stretched.

"I'm okay. I reserve the right to freak out about it later, but for now, I'm good."

"Athena said there's ensuites in all the rooms. Let's go get cleaned up, yeah?"

I couldn't remember Athena saying anything of the sort, maybe it was one of the things they'd been texting about, like the keypad at the door.

Gage lifted me in his arms like a princess and carried me to the ensuite. It was hidden behind the wall of riding crops, and it was a very nice, modern bathroom.

Gage didn't leave my side once, always touching me in some way. He helped me clean up in the shower, dried me off with one of the plush towels provided and then we went back into the room to get dressed again.

23

GAGE

It would take a few more feedings before we had our connection back to where it was. But there was something more there now than there had been.

On the drive home Brand had started to nod off. I was fully prepared to carry him right up to the apartment, but he woke up and fought me off.

"I can walk."

"Then I didn't do my job right." I teased, feeling goofy but being rewarded by his smile.

I took the collar off him when we got back inside.

He pouted.

"You want to keep it on? I thought you weren't into the 24/7 life thing." I dangled the collar in front of him.

"I'm not. But I got used to how it felt." He rubbed his neck.

A wave of affection flooded my chest.

He looked up, his pout turning into a pleased smile. "I felt that."

"Good." I pulled him in for a kiss, one of pure joy and gratitude that he was mine.

We held onto each other for far longer than we usually

would after a kiss. I basked in his contentment and love and I knew he felt mine as well.

It had been three days, and I'd used some of my blood supply, not wanting to push Brand into feeding on the old schedule too quickly.

I was answering a few work emails and starting to feel peckish when Brand returned from college.

"I'm in here!" I called out.

"Uh huh!"

I heard him moving around the apartment. A thud as he dropped his backpack near the table he'd claimed as a desk. Into the kitchen for a drink, that was all normal.

Then his footsteps moved away, towards the bedroom.

Weird. Maybe he's taking a nap? Kind of strange he wouldn't come and say hi, though.

I didn't want to overthink it. Maybe school had been a lot and he just needed space. I could give that to him easily, now that I knew he was safely home.

Since the incident we'd added each other's phones on an app he'd found so we could track each other's locations. I found it slightly creepy to have tech that did that, but very comforting to know I could double check he hadn't suddenly been kidnapped again.

I was very close to hiring him a bodyguard. In fact I'd had a few shortlisted.

Two days ago, I'd showed him my options on a tablet on the couch. Brand shook his head.

"No way, Gage. I'm not gonna be the weird guy at college with a bodyguard following me everywhere. People are going to think I'm a movie star or some politician's son."

"I'm not seeing a problem with that."

"I just want an ordinary college experience. Well." He pushed his hand through his hair. It was getting shaggy and needed a cut, but I liked the length on him. Good to pull on. "As normal as it can be when I have a sugar daddy vampire boyfriend."

I grinned, running a hand up his thigh. "I could just hire one to tail you and stay out of sight? Then it wouldn't be as weird."

"Please don't?"

He'd given me full puppy dog eyes.

I'd relented. But I still felt the tiniest bit of nerves when he went somewhere without me. I'd have to get over it.

I got back to my work emails and sighed. It was all very boring but certain people had to be kept happy if I wanted to keep making money.

A text came through, making my phone beep. Glad of the distraction, I tapped it to see it was Athena.

Athena: Club play night tomorrow, you coming? We have a couple of Shibari displays and a very fine suspension performance planned

Gage: most likely, yeah

Gage: will have to check B's okay with it but I'm keen

Athena: see you there. Unless I don't, in which case I'll see you at the next one

I sent her a thumbs up emoji and turned back to the screen.

Something bugged me.

I shifted in my seat, unable to get comfortable.

What was that?

I snapped to attention when I realized it was arousal. Not

mine, but Brand's. It tugged at my attention and my body was responding.

"What are you doing?" I called out.

No response.

I closed down my laptop and spun my work chair around. Whatever he was doing, I wanted to be part of it. I guessed watching porn, since he'd gone into the bedroom and hadn't responded.

"Bra-and." I let the word draw out, playful so he'd know I was onto him. "Answer me."

"Just a sec!"

I chuckled. He sounded flustered and a hundred per cent like I'd caught him in the act. But in the act of what?

I'd never told him he couldn't jerk off, but if he was going to why do it in my bedroom?

"Hold on, just...stay right where you are. Please? It'll be worth it."

I rolled my eyes, but once again found myself utterly unable to say no to him. I stopped in the middle of the living room and folded my arms, looking toward the bedroom. The bedroom door was mostly closed, so I couldn't see much of anything.

Brand's arousal had heightened and I was semi-hard now, but I would wait. I'd wait until the end of time for him.

Thankfully it was nothing like so long a wait.

The bedroom door moved. "Close your eyes."

"Brand, what?"

"Do it! I promise you, you won't regret it."

"Ugh." I closed my eyes. Shifted my weight from one foot to the other. I hated waiting. That's why it was so much fun to make Brand wait for things. But if he wanted to surprise me with something sexy, who was I to complain about it?

"This better not take too much longer."

I heard soft padding of feet and smelled Brand close to me. "Open your eyes."

I opened my eyes and my jaw dropped.

Brand had gotten changed. And...waxed?

He stood there, all six foot three of him, clad in the leather booty shorts I'd bought him, the leather harness and collar, and sheer black stockings with little garters that showed below the hem of the shorts.

His legs looked seven miles long, smooth, shapely, and fucking... illegal.

"What do you think?"

I tore my eyes away from his muscular thighs to look at his face as he spoke.

Brand looked shy, his cheeks pink.

He'd pushed his hair back and it was held in place by a headband with black bunny ears on it.

I couldn't speak. I could barely move.

I'd never been so turned on in my life or my un-life.

"Gage?" Brand moved closer, one hand now crossing over his chest to hold his other arm.

Oh god, he thinks you don't like it you have to say something you oaf. Say it now before he changes his mind.

"You. Look. Incredible. No. You look fuckable and delicious and I want to pounce on you and do all sorts of unspeakable things to you."

Brand looked relieved, and dropped his arm, instead putting his hands on his hips. His leather-clad hips.

"Good. I thought this would be a nice surprise."

I moved closer in, stroking one hand up his thigh. It was sleek and the stocking pleasingly silky. Absolutely unholy.

I hooked a finger through the ring on his collar and tugged him in for a kiss, trying to convey all my delight, surprise and arousal, sending it through the link between us as best I knew how.

Brand moaned, his hands going to my waist.

I pressed against him.

"Get into the bedroom, now." I growled.

Brand bounced back, grinning so I saw a dimple in his cheek, absolutely adorable with the bunny ears. Adorable and fuckable at the same time.

"Chase me?" He was off, bounding towards the bedroom full of energy.

I gave chase, but I didn't want to be too intense with the 'hunting' aspect of the chase, didn't want to bring up bad memories, so as I did, I grumbled.

"These kids and their 'chase me', as if I still have the same amount of energy."

Brand laughed outright. He'd dodged to the far side of the bed, keeping it between us as I entered the room.

"You literally have vampire powers. You can't convince me you're tired."

I stalked around the bed towards him. "C'mere you. Pretty bunny boy. Come here and I'll make you cum so hard you scream."

Brand's chest heaved with that promise. Like the good little pet he is, he came to me.

24

BRANDON

Feeling this playful and spontaneous was exhilerating. It was like having my old self back. But better because I don't know if my old self would have been so willing to go and buy bunny ears and stockings that would fit me, let alone wear them. Or get waxed.

Now I figured, why the hell not? I'd only live once.

I moved towards Gage, drawn as if by a magnet. He reached out and took my hands, pulling me in for another kiss, this one just as searing.

My knees buckled.

Gage's hands slid up to my wrists. He tutted against my lips. "Where are your cuffs, pet?"

"I thought you might want to put them on me?" In truth I'd forgotten them, I'd been so excited to show Gage the stockings.

Gage hummed. "On the bed, sit up with your legs out."

I sank onto the mattress and scooted back, hitching my legs up and stretching them out. Gage climbed in between them, his hands roving up and down the stockings. It was an incredibly hot gesture, the silkiness of the stockings made his hands feel different. I loved it.

I moaned as he leaned in to kiss the skin of my thighs, the small bit revealed between stocking and leather shorts.

I wanted him to bite me there, but not yet.

I wanted this to last.

Gage climbed half on top of me, forcing me to lean back against the pillows. "You're gorgeous pet. So fucking gorgeous. What did I do to deserve such a hot thing like you?"

"You're a good person." I leaned up to kiss his jaw. "You deserve everything."

"Ugh, so sappy." Gage playfully shoved my shoulder and I laughed. "Now tell me what made you think of this?"

He pinched some stocking between his thumb and forefinger and pulled it away from my skin.

"I was thinking about how much you liked the shorts on me, and then I just got to thinking about what would go with them, that's all."

Gage hummed and slipped a hand under the stocking and then up. "What's holding these garters up?"

"You'll have to take the shorts off to see."

"Mm. Not ready to do that yet. Roll over."

I did as he said, folding my arms to rest my cheek on them. He stroked his hand over my back, tugging at the harness as he did so, and pulling it tighter on my front. Then he smoothed his hand over my ass, slapping it lightly.

I moaned in response.

Gage chuckled. "You want me to spank you more, pet? Pretty bunny?"

I squirmed at the name. "Yes, please."

He spanked me again, harder this time. The noise his palm made against the leather was incredible. He spanked both cheeks solidly until I was squirming, rutting against the bed. I could feel his arousal and it spiked mine higher.

"Lift your hips."

I complied and Gage reached around to undo the shorts and

pull them down my legs. I hid my face, knowing he'd see the silky black garter belt I'd fumbled on in order to hold up the stockings.

Gage's arousal skyrocketed and I moaned, feeling hard and needy.

"Brand you dirty whore. Look at you."

He slapped my ass again.

I jolted. Without the leather protecting me the blow smarted more. "You like it then?"

He leaned in and bit my ass. Not enough to feed, just enough to have me moaning.

He pulled back to grumble. "Gonna give me a heart attack and he asks if I like it. For the love of..."

"Your heart doesn't go, you can't have a heart attack."

Gripping my hips, Gage flipped me over onto my back. "Pull the pillows up, get comfortable. I want to fuck you with your legs wrapped around me so I can feel everything."

I did as he said, pulling all the pillows behind and under me and tilting my pelvis so he had a better angle, and settled back.

Meanwhile Gage had retrieved my leather cuffs. He knelt between my legs and reached for my hands to cuff me.

I pressed my thighs against his hips and tried not to pant too hard just from the act of him tying me up. It'd never get sick of it.

"Hmm." He tugged me forward to lean against his chest. "I think this harness has... yes."

He pulled my arms behind me and folded them, so my forearms pressed against each other horizontally. He clipped the cuffs to the harness securing my arms behind me. He leaned me gently back down on the pillows.

"There, pretty boy. Feel comfortable?"

"Surprisingly, yes."

He smirked and kissed me. "Love having you bound up for me, it's so hot." He kissed his way down my neck and chest, making me squirm more. "And this?" He took the garter belt between his teeth, tugged it and let it snap back against me.

I jolted even though it barely hurt. I was on edge from all the build up. He could have tugged my earlobe and I'd be close to orgasm.

"You're a minx, Brand. And up until I saw you in these I thought that was something only girls could be."

I flushed, always susceptible to his dirty talk. "I remembered, ages ago, you were talking about lingerie..."

He leaned in and licked a stripe up my cock. "Yes, I did. Maybe we ought to go shopping again? Because this is very much doing it for me."

I tipped my head back. The bunny ears headband gave up and slipped off my head, but I didn't care about that. The stockings were clearly the winner today.

Gage took me in his mouth and with one lubed hand started to stretch me at the same time. He pulled back when he'd stretched me to two fingers and I was whining and panting.

"How many times do you think I can make you come?"

"Like, in my whole life?" I panted.

"In the next hour?"

I groaned, closing my eyes and imagining him wringing orgasm after orgasm out of me. The idea wasn't without appeal but something in me panicked at the idea of being pushed to the edge. "Not... super keen on that idea today."

Gage kissed the inside of my thigh. "Good boy, good boundaries."

He went back to sucking my dick.

I bit my lip to keep from groaning too loudly.

He slipped another finger in.

I started begging.

"Please Gage — Master — Daddy. Please fuck me, I'm ready I know I am and I need to feel you fill me so badly. Please!"

"Always beg so pretty." Gage pulled his fingers out and got into position between my legs. He pulled my legs in around his waist and I crossed them at the ankles. "Little fucking sexdoll minx."

He pushed inside.

He must have been in a rush because there was so much lube on him I felt it leak out. There was a distinct squelching sound but I didn't even care. He felt incredible inside me.

"Thank you!"

"Haven't even started yet, pet."

He put one hand on my collar, holding me in place and with his other hand he stroked up and down my thigh.

"Feels so good." My arms twitched, I wanted to pull him in closer. I settled for tightening my legs to bring him deeper inside.

He groaned, rolled his hips. "Yeah it does. Gonna make you feel so good baby, reward you for going to all this effort for me. Bet you had to go buy these in a shop didn't you? That must have been humiliating."

I'd been so close to buying them off Amazon and not caring about the size, but in the end I'd wanted to try on the belt at least. "Yeah. I did."

Gage chuckled darkly. "Would have liked to see that."

"Why?" I knew the answer, but I wanted to hear his filthy talk.

"See you squirm, get all red and needy, embarrassed by how much you want to be embarrassed."

My moan was guttural.

"Love it don't you? Love to be put in your place and demeaned. Well. I can help with that."

He closed his hand over my throat.

I tensed.

It didn't exactly remind me of Shawna, but it was close.

"Check in?"

I took a deep breath. "Orange...didn't like the talk... but I'll be green in a second just give me..."

He stopped moving, giving me time to adjust and get myself together.

I raked my eyes over him. This was Gage. My Gage, who would stop if I told him to.

I was safe.

I didn't need to stop. "Green."

Gage tightened his grip on my throat. It wasn't enough to stop my breath, just enough to remind me that he could if he wanted to. I was bound up, I couldn't stop him.

My body squeezed and clenched, already close to coming.

"Tell me what you're thinking, pet. I can feel how hot you are."

He loosened his grip on my neck.

"I just love being yours, being helpless for you. Knowing you could do anything to me, it's so hot. Love being your ..." What was the word he'd used just before? "Minx."

He chuckled, thrusting harder now and hitting my prostate just right. "Good boy. My good little submissive pet."

I shuddered, gasping. "Please Sir?"

"Come for me."

A few more thrusts and then I was there, flooded with endorphins and bucking so he was plunged deeper inside. He hadn't even had to stroke my dick, his hand on the stockings and his words were enough.

In a moment he was coming too, his hips thrusting erratically and shuddering to a stop. He sprawled over his chest, his mouth on my collarbone. "So good."

"You didn't bite..." I realized a beat too late.

Gage rubbed his thumb on my cheek. "Don't need to."

"But I want it."

He grumbled again, sitting up and slipping out of me at the

same moment. I let my legs fall to the mattress on either side of him. "Well, if you want it..."

"On my thigh." I was still bound so I nodded down. "Where the skin is exposed."

Gage's eyes darkened and he moved into position. "Such a dirty whore for me. I love it."

He wrapped a hand around my calf and lifted my leg, leaning the rest of the way in to fasten his mouth over the tender skin of my thigh. He kissed it first, then licked, teasing me. I was spent but my dick twitched, unable to withstand the eroticism of watching him there.

Finally he popped his fangs and bit down.

"Ah!" It never hurt much with Gage, but that was a particularly sensitive area and I was already hyper sensitive. The sting immediately melted into pleasure and my dick hardened entirely.

I watched Gage, his hair falling forward onto his face as he drank down from the large vein in my thigh. It felt like being stroked. Like being fucked. Like all my erogenous zones were being activated at once.

"Fuck yeah." He chuckled, a trickle of my blood leaked out the side of his mouth. He licked the wound clean.

"You love it so much."

"Yeah, I do." I breathed out. My dick was softening again, it had just been too soon. "When you do it."

"When I do it. And no one else is ever going to." He kissed the place he'd bitten and climbed up to wrap me in his arms, undoing the cuffs so I could hold him. "I love you, Brand."

"Love you." I nuzzled into him and relaxed entirely. No place in the world was safer than his arms.

25

BRANDON

"I can't believe you're skipping out on me before the semester is even over," Max teased. "How am I going to find another roommate? You're killing me here."

He'd made this joke a dozen times, and I'd responded a different way every time. "Yeah, well, you just don't fuck me the way Gage does."

Max burst out laughing and I joined in.

Martina came back into the room for another box. "What are you two laughing about?"

I just about bit my tongue. "Nothing."

Max raised his eyebrows and busied himself with picking up my surfboard. "Don't be a stranger, okay?"

"Of course not." My mood deepened and I went to pat his shoulder. "We'll still do lunch and go surfing and everything."

Max set my board down and gave me a hug.

"Oh my god, you two. It's not like Brand is moving to another country." Martina laughed fondly.

I squeezed Max against my chest. I knew it was probably an overreaction, but I was really going to miss him. I was afraid our relationship would change.

Max pulled back finally. "Stay gold, Ponyboy."

"Oh my fucking *god!*" Martina pelted us with couch cushions.

I laughed, putting some space between us.

"Okay, we're done, we're done!"

Gage had paid for the moving van. He'd offered to pay for movers as well, but I didn't have that much stuff to bring over, so I said I'd do it myself. Now I was glad I had, since Max seemed to be enjoying our time together. Martina's being in town on moving day was a happy coincidence.

I went into my old room to check I hadn't left anything behind. The bed and mattress and side table that had come with the place were the only things still left in the room.

I looked around, drinking it all in. My college apartment. I'd had some good memories in this place, some not so good ones as well. All those meaningless hookups, looking for something I could have never guessed I needed — a vampire dom. A Master.

I said a quiet thank you to the room and went back into the living space. Max was holding my board and Martina had a bag of stuff from the kitchen.

"Okay, I think that's pretty much everything." I picked up my backpack, stuffed with my essentials — school books, laptop, phone charger. "I won't need any help at the other end. Gage has a couple of his friends to help unload."

We went down together and packed the last stuff into the van. Martina hugged me tight and kissed my cheek. "Text me later. And remember you can always change your mind and we'll move you right back in."

"I know." I squeezed her. "But I won't."

"Gage is a good guy, but you just never know someone until you're living with them." Martina looked me square in the eye. "He might surprise you."

I grinned. "He already has."

They waved me off as I pulled the van into traffic and headed towards Gage's building. If I looked into the rear view mirror and teared up a little, well. No one knew but me.

Gage brought the last load up.

"I already called the company. They're gonna come and collect the van." He set the box down in the spare room which was now designated mine.

It was easily three times the size of my room at the old place and he'd already bought a massive bed for me, complete with a headboard designed to have multiple bondage points. The room had a walk-in wardrobe and an ensuite. I felt like I was in a fancy hotel.

I was hanging the last of my shirts up. The stuff Gage had bought me was already hanging there, along with some I didn't recognize. He must have gone shopping again.

"I don't even know how much I'm gonna use this room."

"You'd better use that desk." Gage pointed to the sit/stand adjustable desk in the corner. "For your homework. Besides, I want you to have your own space. Sometimes you'll want alone time. Sometimes I might want alone time. It sounds crazy but it's true."

I walked over to him, chest bursting with nervous excitement. He slipped his arms around me. I rested my chin on his head.

"Don't do that. It makes me feel short."

"You are short."

He tickled my side and I straightened up a bit but didn't let go. "You okay, puppy?"

"Yeah just feeling... a lot today."

"Big change."

"Yeah. My sister's standing offer to kick your ass seems to be still in play, by the way."

Gage chuckled. "Martina's so cool. I am warned and duly intimidated." He leaned back to look me in the eye. "Anything you need?"

"Yeah. Dinner."

Gage laughed. "Anything you want, babe."

"Steak." I grinned. "It's good for my iron levels. Side of garlic butter and some leafy green veggies, fries, a banana split and the biggest coke you can buy."

Gage shook his head and laughed some more. "You got it. Eat in or go out?"

"I just got here, I want to eat in. And watch some trashy action movies. And cuddle."

"I did say anything you wanted. Get settled in and I'll order dinner."

I kissed his nose and he batted me away, phone already out as he sauntered back into the living area.

I looked around my new room. I felt good about this choice, and I was looking forward to settling into the room, and making a proper space for myself in Gage's life. But it still felt like a huge step to have taken.

Still, it wasn't like I'd agreed to be turned into a vampire or something.

My phone buzzed. I remembered I was supposed to text Martina.

I blinked at the message on my phone.

I didn't have the number saved, and the text wasn't exactly friendly.

Unknown number: you got away for now, but this isn't over. Gage will be mine again, and you're going to help me little pet

"Gage!" My heart thudded and I struggled to take a breath. "We might have a problem!"

To be continued...

ALSO BY DRAKE

NIGHT'S MELODY - MONSTERS AND MAYHEM

Buy Now

he opera house holds many secrets, but none are as frightening as the Opera Ghost.

Matthieu has harboured a crush on his best friend, Christophe, since they started dancing together in the Paris opera ballet troupe, but he's never acted on it.

When disaster strikes only hours before a gala performance, Christophe reveals a hidden talent for singing.

But where did he learn to hit such beautiful high notes? Why won't he tell his best friend who his singing tutor is? And what are those bruises he's covering up?

. . .

The rehearsals for their new opera are plagued with "accidents" and a dashing stranger who has a past connection with the beautiful Christophe disrupts their lives. To make matters worse, Matthieu seems to have attracted the attention of the Phantom of the Opera himself... but who is the man behind the mask? And why is he so very alluring?

The melody heard in the darkest part of the night is terrible, but beautiful as well.

Night's Melody is an MM horror retelling of the Phantom of the Opera, as part of the collaboration Monsters & Mayhem: An MM Horror Collection, adapting some of your favourite classic horror stories with an MM romance twist.

It is a standalone story, featuring accidents of a violent nature, overdramatic characters, why choose/ MMMM scenes and some very intriguing torture chambers under the opera's stage floor.

ALSO BY DRAKE

GARDEN OF SECRETS - MISSELTHWAITE BOOK ONE

Buy Now

Alistair Lennox is disagreeable.

Isolated and miserable, with parents who don't care about him, his life has been equal parts privilege and loneliness.

But when his parents die, his life is turned upside down. In order to gain his inheritance, Alistair is forced to attend a college he's never heard of - for good reason. Misselthwaite College is a school for the magically gifted

Alistair has no magical gifts - unless being magically inept counts. What were his parents thinking? And what is the mysterious affliction plaguing William Carlisle, the affluent and arrogant heir to Misselthwaite? Is there a connection to the strange key Alistair discovers in a book, the stranger noises in the night, and, strangest of all, the multiple men who desire his friendship? Misselthwaite has no end of secrets.

But if being disagreeable is good for anything, it's for getting to the bottom of mysteries.

--

Garden of Secrets is book one in a duology, and the first installment in a magical new universe. A Secret Garden retelling with a queer twist and featuring MMMM polyamory.

MORE BY DRAKE

HIS PIRATICAL HAREM BOOK 1 – CABIN BOY
BY DRAKE LAMARQUE

Buy now

I've never been what I was supposed to be. Wealthy sons of Port Governors aren't supposed to be ejected from the British Navy after less than a year, they're not supposed to like pulp romances or daydream about the handsome heroes of the stories instead of the heroines.

When my Father issued me an order to marry a woman, I knew I had no choice but to make my own way in the world, and I found a berth on the first ship out of Jamaica.

I didn't mean to join a pirate ship, and I certainly didn't intend to find myself the cabin boy to an incredibly charming Pirate Captain. Or that I'd also be attracted to the mysterious First Mate, or that both of them would show me all sorts of unspeakable and salacious pleasures while on board. How can I choose just one of them when I want both?

In addition to confusion on board the ship, there's also enchanting genderfluid merfolk, a cat which seems to understand a lot more than it should, an unseasonable storm and a sea witch with a serious grudge... and with all these complications, I am definitely in over my head.

Come and meet the crew:

Gideon: an innocent with a lot of forbidden desires and a lot of love to give

Tate: a huge, muscular ship's captain with a sweet side

Ezra: a dominant and closed off first mate

Ora: a genderqueer, curious and affectionate merman

This spicy MMMMM series is complete and available on KU

MORE BY DRAKE

GENTLEMAN'S BOUNTY BOOK 1 - KIDNAPPED BY THE GENTLEMAN BY DRAKE LAMARQUE

Buy Now

Cedric has been kidnapped by pirates.

...they have no idea how much trouble they're in for.

Cedric was living his best life, partying in the colonies, bedding whomever he pleased and trusting that his parents' money and affluence would get him out of any unfortunate scrapes.

Until he was kidnapped by the fearsome pirate Lucifer, who planned to trade him for a hefty ransom. Unfortunately, he's not the only one after Cedric, and the strange secret society who have Cedric in their sights might just be more dangerous than Captain Lucifer.

Now Cedric is trapped on a pirate ship with a dashingly handsome captain, a quartermaster who won't stop staring at him and an overwhelming desire to find some fun, all while saving his hide from an unknown organisation who will stop at nothing to track him down.

This spicy MMMM series is complete and available on KU

Buy now

There are three golden rules for new recruits at Fairyland Theme Park:

1. No breaking character, even if you're dying of heat exhaustion
2. Always give guests the most magical time
3. No falling in love.

Nate's only been at work one day, and he's already broken all three.

Fast-tracked into a Prince role, Nate's at odds with Dash, the handsome not-so-charming prince who is supposed to be training him. Nate doesn't know how he ended up on Dash's bad side, but the broody prince sure is hot when he gets mad.

Dash has worked long and hard to play Prince Justice at Fairyland. Now, instead of focusing on his own performance, he is forced to train newbie Nate to be the perfect prince. Nate's annoying ease with the guests coupled with his charm and good looks could dethrone Dash from his number one spot ... so why does he secretly want to kiss him?

Fairyland heats up as sparks fly between the two rival princes. Will they get their fairytale romance before they're kicked out of Fairyland for good?

Find out in this standalone MM contemporary romance by Jaxon Knight, set in an amusement park where fairytales can come true.

ALSO PUBLISHED BY GREY KELPIE STUDIO

OVERDUES AND OCCULTISM BY JAMIE SANDS

Busy now

A witch in the broom closet probably shouldn't be so interested in a ghost hunter, right?

That Basil is a librarian comes as no surprise to his Mt Eden community. That he's a witch? Yeah. That might raise more than a few eyebrows.

When Sebastian, a paranormal investigator filming a web series starts snooping around Basil's library, he stirs up more than just Basil's heart.

Between Basil's own self-doubt, a ghost who steals books and Sebastian, an enthusiastic extrovert bent on uncovering secrets, Basil's life is about to get a lot more complicated.

Overdues and Occultism is a sweet, no heat contemporary novella about a witch living in Auckland, New Zealand. MM romance, HEA.